ADVANCE PRAISE FOR
TO SEE THE SUMMER SKY

family's adventure. The character development throughout the series and attention to detail by D.M. Herrmann is unmatched by other authors. I eagerly await *Fire of Death* and would be pleased to see a film adaptation of this series in the future."

—Clint E.,
Chief Warrant Officer Three, United States Army

"D.M. Herrmann's third installment of his John Henry Chronicles takes us to the post-apocalyptic aftermath of an electromagnetic burst that leaves the survivors bewildered, dazed and disorganized. Tribalism reigns. It is every man for himself, where the bonds of family face off against the remnants of government power in a struggle for supremacy."

—Charles DuPuy,
Author of the EZ Kelly Mystery series

TO SEE THE SUMMER SKY

D.M. Herrmann

TO SEE THE SUMMER SKY

Book Three of the John Henry Chronicles

D.M. Herrmann

Green Bay, WI 54311

To See the Summer Sky: **A John Henry Chronicles Novel** by D.M. Herrmann, © 2021 by D.M. Herrmann. Author photo courtesy of the Herrmann family.

Publisher/Executive Editor: Brittiany Koren
Cover Art Designer: Ed Vincent/ENC Graphics
Interior Layout Designer: Amit Dey
Ebook Interior Layout Designer: Amit Dey

Category: Post-apocalyptic Military Science Fiction
Description: Following a catastrophic event, the Henry family struggles to survive and rebuild in Wisconsin in a continuation of the novel series.

Hard Cover ISBN: 978-1-951375-59-1
Paperback ISBN: 978-1-951375-60-7
Ebook ISBN: 978-1-951375-61-4
LOC Catalogue Data: Applied for.

First Edition published by Written Dreams Publishing in November, 2021.

Green Bay, WI 54311

ALSO BY
D.M. HERRMANN

Innisfree, Book One
of the John Henry Chronicles
Their Star Is Their World, Book Two
of the John Henry Chronicles
To See the Summer Sky, Book Three
of the John Henry Chronicles

BOOKS WRITTEN
AS EVAN MICHAEL MARTIN

Sorceress Rising, Book 1,
A Clio Boru Story
Sorceress Revealed, Book 2,
A Clio Boru Story
Sorceress Resurrected, Book 3,
A Clio Boru Story

NOTE FROM THE AUTHOR

This is a work of fiction, or is it. Much of what you will read here is either true or fact. Of course, the characters and the storyline are not.

The story contains information that anyone wanting to be prepared could use. But that isn't the main purpose of this story. The story is about people. People who call themselves family. More than biological family it is about how people come together and become family. Through deed and circumstance, they form a bond.

This is the story of one such man. Divorced and living apart from all of his family he struggles during a time of enormous crisis to bring them together, keep them together and also protect them. He longs for peace, and the dream of a forest glade, where he is safe, and so are they. He faces the reality of great evil and the natural tendencies of man. This is the struggle of all who cherish their families; this is the struggle of John Henry.

This book is dedicated to families, families together, families apart, families created by circumstance. Families are drawn together for good and bad, families driven apart because of words. Families reunited because of hurt. Cherish those families, regardless of where you are. The family is the very root of our existence.

Some may find parts of the story disturbing. It should be. However, all of the so-called experts agree that our civilization on any given day is about 3-days away from completely breaking down if the right circumstances occur. The inability to provide the necessities of life will quickly degenerate, and as the animals that humans are, the violent tendencies we all naturally have will return then if for no other reason than to survive. Unlike some books in this genre, this story contains profanity. I felt it was a more accurate portrayal of life in stressful times and did not want to paint an inaccurate or unrealistic picture of the environment. Much of what you can learn in this book can be put to use to help your family survive and possibly thrive in any short or long-term breakdown of essential services or society. We've seen it following hurricanes, both the good and the bad.

Fair warning, this book has several graphic scenes that may upset some people. The scenes are used to show how low human behavior can go when society breaks down.

So enjoy the story, enjoy the will and struggle to survive during challenging, terrible times. So in the words of a childhood cartoon character... Let's get dangerous!

"To see the Summer Sky
Is Poetry, though never in a
Book it lie—True Poems flee—".

—Emily Dickinson

To my readers,
You make writing enjoyable, and your
enthusiasm for these stories
fuels my efforts. Thank you!

And to L.H. You keep it going.

PROLOGUE

"Shhhh," the man said. His heavy bearded younger partner peered into the thick brush ahead. The rustle of the leaves and branches told them their quarry was near. The two men lay on the ground and didn't move. The rustling intensified as they waited, their heart beats picking up speed as the excitement of the moment was driven by extra adrenalin coursing through their bodies.

"BAM," the single shot from the older bearded man's rifle rang out through the forest.

A crash, and then silence followed.

A quick glance between the two men and then they exclaimed together, "WOO HOO!"

Jumping to their feet, the two men moved slowly over to the tan and white mass lying on the ground. The shooter reached his rifle forward and tapped the deer's eye. When the deer didn't move, he said, "He's dead."

The hunting partners stood there for a moment letting the adrenaline rush subside.

"Good shot," the older man said to his youthful, bearded partner. "If you'd have missed, Emma would never had let you live it down."

"Yeah, Sweetie would have busted my chops for days. Young as she is, that girl can bring down the disapproval over anyone's shooting ability better than someone much older."

"You gonna tell her about her grandpa?"

"Of course. Just trying to figure out how best to tell the story, the one that is so hard to tell."

"She'll learn it from somebody. Better it comes from you. After all, you're her dad."

CHAPTER 1

"To be prepared for war is one of the most effective means of preserving peace."

—George Washington

It had been a few months since the EMP started what would bring us all to this point—living in a world without electricity, vehicles, or computers. As the head of this group, I found keeping the family informed of what was happening to be sometimes a less than pleasant experience. I'm John Henry, and my story continues.

As was our custom, we met on the porch of the large cabin in Lakeview, Wisconsin. It had become our "living room" in the nicer weather months of the year. Those days would be ending soon, in about six to eight weeks I figured, before the days started getting chilly.

For the "Big Picture" talks, I liked for everyone to get together and hear it one time, ask questions, and discuss any issues. Then I knew everyone had the same information.

I didn't hold too much back in those meetings, unless the kids were present. Much of what was coming was a bit intense for them, and they didn't need to hear it. Their lives had been disrupted enough, although the three boys had almost gone "feral" and were adapting to our new way of life quite nicely.

Mike, my grandson, was the only one who had strong memories of before the EMP. He still missed playing his video games online with his friends.

Linda's boys, Ethan and Caleb, were young enough that their memories weren't as clear, or as my son, Chief Brian Henry, had said once, their addiction was not as developed.

"Okay, everyone, listen up," I began. "Trouble is coming…"

"What's new?" Chris Rahn said. "It's always trouble anymore."

First Sergeant Chris Rahn and a few men of his had their permanent residence here. They had moved into a cabin that was built on my land near the big cabin.

"No shit," Craig Henry replied. Being my youngest son, Craig didn't hold back his opinions. Today he was uncustomarily alone as Addie was on guard in the bunker, and Gary Jones, our resident former marine, was out back watching the field.

We'd have to move that guard point soon as it was too close to the new cabins to be of any value to us. We now had five, counting the two cabins that would be finished in another day or so. They were beginning to block our view of the field and woods behind the main cabin.

Brian wanted to build a tower closer to the field or even in the tree line. I nixed that idea, because we didn't have the communications wire to string a phone that far. It would have to be something closer in. I didn't think a tower was a good idea, either.

"It's too big of a target and too far out to get help if it's needed," I told him.

He didn't like my answer.

"Okay, everyone. Listen up," I said to the family situated around me on the porch. "Sam and I were on the Ham."

"Sam on the Ham," Brian quipped.

"Knock it off, Brian. Things are going to get real serious," I replied.

His soldiers, all standing around or sitting by the steps, chuckled at Chief Henry being told what to do.

"May I continue," I said, glaring at Brian and then his men.

"Sorry, Dad," he said.

"As I was saying, Sam and I were on the Ham."

Brian stared at his feet, and I knew he was getting ready to be a smart ass. He kept his mouth shut.

"Seems FEMA is going to come looking for us and their leader, Major Wolfe, is of a mind to take no prisoners."

"He's not their leader, John. They have a FEMA guy, a Captain Jamison. Real hard case. He's in charge. Wolfe is probably just there because he knows the area," Rahn interjected.

"Anyway," I continued. My irritation at being interrupted was starting to show.

"What does 'take no prisoners' mean, John?" Linda Haines asked.

"Folks, please, we can save the questions till after I explain what is happening," I snapped.

Then, realizing that unlike the rest of us, Linda didn't have direct military experience, probably didn't know what that meant, and if she did, she had two little boys to worry about, so I explained.

"Exactly what it sounds like. No prisoners, no survivors," I said probably a bit too bluntly.

Her hand went to her mouth as she took in what that meant.

Way to go, John. Scaring people is not what you should be doing right now.

"Major Wolfe," I continued, giving Rahn one of my don't interrupt me, please looks, "said he is coming for us and plans to destroy us. It seems he didn't like me too much, either. That means we must step up our game here a bit."

I stopped and let my eyes travel across everyone that was present. I had their attention.

"Brian, I know you have roving patrols out, and that will continue for quite a while. We are not alone, either."

Brian started to say something, thought better of it and kept silent.

I gave him a dad smile and continued. "An old U.S. Army friend, Peter Corn from the Rez, is sending some people over here to help with the patrols. They'll be on horseback and will be staying here. They'll patrol the back roads and logging trails, as well as help with the Hummer patrols."

"Boy, that's a switch. Indians rescuing the settlers," Brian quickly remarked.

I couldn't get mad at that one even if he didn't say it politically correct as it helped lessen the intensity of my words and relaxed everyone a bit. He got another look anyway.

"So, we'll have the nine soldiers plus Rahn and our people, and about ten or so from the Rez. That's roughly about forty people in total. I wish we had more. Maybe we can reach out to the few that stayed out here and the Winstons for help. After the Winstons' little run-in with a couple of the FEMA boys and Charlie's visit here the other day, I think they'll be in with us. I don't see them taking orders from any of us, though."

"Besides the patrols, what do you want us to do?" Brian asked.

"We have to accept the fact that people are going to get hurt, or worse," I answered. "We need to be ready to take care of our injured," I said, avoiding the word wounded for some reason, "and be ready with other plans, to include evacuating if we have to. Donna, could you and Linda start inventorying our medical supplies and see what we have on hand for bandages, herbs, and things like that? I'll ask Peter if he has any meds or related items that he could donate to the cause."

"That won't be a problem," Donna said. "The big thing will be pain killers and antibiotics."

"I'm sure Peter has access to something to be used as a painkiller. Antibiotics will probably be impossible, so if you or Linda know of any herbal remedies, please don't hesitate to make them, get them, or whatever it is you have to do."

"We've got herbs in the garden that can be used for some things. Honey is always good. Maybe we could find a wild hive somewhere, and if someone can find some wild garlic or raid some of the gardens people left behind that would help, too," she added.

"Good. Those are the kinds of things we need to do. Nancy, can you inventory our dried food and divide some of the rice and beans out? I want to set up some caches in case we need to bug out. No sense in starving too much if we lose what we have here."

"You think it will come to that, FIL?" she asked, using her nickname for me.

"I don't know, but I hope not. If it does, I want to be prepared. That means we'll have to stash weapons and ammo, too. Chris, how are we set for ammo and explosives?"

"We're good, John. We've got almost 250,000 rounds of 5.56, about a dozen cases of grenades, too many MREs and roughly 25 or 30 claymores."

"I'm surprised you don't know the exact number," I joked.

Rahn grinned. "We're still inventorying. My guys did good at requisitioning extras. We'll also pick up more along the way."

"Where will you get more from?" Linda asked.

"From the FEMA boys who won't need them anymore, Ma'am," he answered, nodding his head at her.

"What? Oh, never mind. I understand," she said.

The FEMA troops we killed or ran off wouldn't need weapons or ammo. We'd pick it up off of the battlefields as they occurred. It wasn't an ideal solution, but it was all we had.

"Any more questions?" I asked.

Rahn gave a good first sergeant glare to his men to silence them, and I made eye contact with everyone else.

"Okay then, it looks like we have our work cut out for us. Brian, Chris, could you stay, please?" I asked.

"You betchya," Brian replied.

Rahn rolled his eyes. "What is it with this 'you betchya' shit?" he said. Then, a moment later, he shouted, "Johnson."

"Yes, First Sergeant," the young soldier replied.

"Get with Craig and Sam, grab a couple of guys, as many as you need, and get those cabins finished. Pronto."

"You betchya, First Sergeant," a grinning Specialist Johnson replied.

"Don't start with me," Rahn said. "That's not how you answer a First Sergeant."

"Yes, First Sergeant."

"Specialist Hart," Rahn shouted. "Finish the inventory, and then start putting together scout teams. We'll talk about schedules and routes later.

"Hooah, First Sergeant."

"That's a good reply. Did you hear that, Johnson?" Rahn asked.

"Hooah, First Sergeant," the still grinning specialist answered.

Everyone went about their business. Brian and Rahn pulled their chairs over and sat down near me.

"Well, the shits about to get real," I remarked. "What are your thoughts?"

For the next half hour, the three of us talked about strategy and planned as best we could.

CHAPTER 2

"Beware the Jabberwock, my son."

—Lewis Carroll

Captain Roy Jamison, FEMA Quick Reaction Force (QRF), was a tall, sandy-haired man of medium build. He stood in the office he had commandeered from Major Elias Wolfe studying a map board that had been placed on an easel. The map was a military-style topographical map that showed all of the territory between Antigo and Markton. The area he now referred to as Indian Country.

The irony was not lost on Jamison as the land south of Markton and extending west about 16 miles to just south of Polar was an area he had explicitly been told to stay out of—the Menominee Indian Reservation. He knew they would deal with "those people" later.

Wearing his standard all-black uniform—he liked to believe it projected an aura of authority—Jamison rocked back and forth on his heels, his eyes focused on something in the map. He also knew it scared the hell out of a lot of people. The appearance of someone in his door took his attention away from it.

Turning to face the door he said, "Oh, come in, Elias."

Major Elias Wolfe was a young-looking U.S. Army National Guard infantry officer. Standing about six feet tall, he had tight curly brown hair and an infectious smile that was as deceptive as it was warm. Elias Wolfe had shown he could at least project an air of cruelty that drew Jamison to liking him. While Jamison felt the major was a bit of a wimp and would sell his mother to get ahead, he still believed Wolfe had potential. Potential that he would use to accomplish the mission he had been brought here to accomplish by Rick Barstow, the FEMA Regional Administrator in Wausau.

Major Wolfe entered the room, his usually starched and pressed ACUs or Army Combat Uniform looking mussed and disheveled after a few days away from the main camp in Wausau. "Good morning, Roy," he said.

"Come look at the map," Roy replied.

Wolfe came closer to the map board, put his hands behind him in the small of his back, and studied it.

"Where is the town of Lake View?" Jamison asked.

"Right about here," Wolfe responded, pointing to a spot not far south from White Lake.

"Dinky little place, it's not even on the map," Jamison said.

"I've not been there, but I hear it's little more than a couple of buildings—a bar, diner, and a gas station."

"My scouts who got their asses ambushed said most of that is burned down," Jamison said testily. "Where do you think this Henry compound is, Elias?"

"I'm not certain," Wolfe answered as he rocked back and forth on his heels. "If you follow the timeline from when the scout team was ambushed and when we estimate their reinforcements showed up, it has to be less than ten or fifteen miles from town."

"How far do you think they are from the Menominee Reservation?" Jamison asked.

"Probably about the same, fifteen miles tops."

"So we can establish a grid of about fifteen miles by fifteen miles and search every inch of it until we find them. I think that should clear this up in a few days, don't you?"

"Yeah, that should work. When do you want us to go out?" Wolfe asked.

"Soon, Elias, soon. Patience."

*   *   *

It took a full day and a half to complete the new cabins and put roofs on them. All that remained was putting the wood stoves in each half of the dog trot design, and for that, we had to find two more stoves. Brian and Rahn had begun to send out patrols and were tasked with exploring the abandoned properties in the area. Hopefully, it'd be easy finding new wood stoves as well as the chimney piping needed. It was while these patrols were out that the excitement began.

I was standing in the hall of the main cabin, mostly daydreaming when the rattle of the field phone made me jump.

"Hello," I answered the call.

"John, this is Addie in the bunker. Your friends are here," she announced.

My heart skipped a beat. "Which friends?"

I guess I snapped those words too sharply because she said, "Sorry, your friends from the reservation. There are ten of them here, with a lot of horses."

"Awesommmme!" I replied, drawing out the end of the word. I left the cabin and headed toward the bunker.

Addie had already waved them in, and the group was coming into view through the trees as I entered the front yard.

"John Henry!" The man in the front of the group shouted as he picked up the pace on his horse and trotted toward me.

He looked familiar, but if it was who I thought, it had been many years since I last set eyes on him. "Is that you, Jake?" I asked in a questioning and uncertain tone. He looked like an older version of Jacob Kook, Peter Corn's nephew.

"You betchya der hey," he said with a laugh, swinging his right leg across the neck of the horse he was riding. Jake Kook hopped down, and with his hand extended, walked the brief few steps toward me.

"Well, I'll be damned," I said. "You grew up. I haven't seen you in almost forever."

"Don't say that too loud, John. You might end up damned," he replied jovially as we shook hands.

"Too bad we had to meet again like this," I said, waving my arm across the property.

"What? This? You've lived here for quite a while; nothing has changed."

"Your dripping sarcasm is noted," I replied with a grin. "So, how many of you are here? Horses, shit, we've got to get you guys set up. I wasn't expecting you so soon."

"Counting me, I have ten men. We each have a horse and a remount. I'm guessing we have about a week's worth of oats packed on them," he answered.

"We can take care of that. I promised your uncle we'd provide feed for the horses, and of course, feed you guys, too. How does pemmican sound? That's what you eat, isn't it?"

The quizzical look on his face caught me off guard, and then, with a slight twinkle in his eye, he remarked, "Nope, we eat buffalo now. Healthier, less cholesterol, and more protein."

"Fresh out," I said.

We stood there for a second, and then Jake reached out, slapped me on the shoulder, and said, "Uncle Peter said you were still a lot of fun."

"Let's get your horses corralled and figure out where in the hell I'm going to put you guys up. We converted some of the stalls in the barn into bunk rooms."

"Well, I heard you were building cabins, John. How many do you have?"

"We've built five dog trots, each with an eight by ten room on each side. The inn is full. We have the room and the start of a village. If you want to, we can build another cabin or two. It would be cramped, but it would house all of you," I offered.

"Let's see how long this plays out," Jake replied. "If it looks like it will go through winter, then hell yeah, we'll want the cabin. I ain't sleeping in a barn in January."

"Sounds good. Let's get this done, and we can talk. I need to get you guys introduced to everyone."

We walked across the yard toward the barn. Once we cleared the house, the five new cabins came into view.

"Damn, John, you building an outpost here?" Jake asked as we continued walking.

"People keep showing up, the main cabin is filled, and they need a place to stay. Everyone can't live in the barn."

"You cut all those logs to build those?" he asked.

"Nope, just some. Most of those came from that logging operation your uncle and I tried to stop. Guess it did turn into a good thing. We're lucky we still have fuel for chain saws, my truck, and the sawmill. Still have a fair amount, but we won't last through winter at the pace we are using it."

"Lots of abandoned gas stations, John. Scavenging is the new shopping."

"The Qwik Mart in town still has gas, and we tap into that occasionally. With our building problem, we'll have to figure out a better way. That could become a battleground. Speaking of a battleground," I said as we came upon Rahn and a couple of soldiers outside the barn observing one of the new motorcycles they had reconstructed. "Chris!"

Chris Rahn, first sergeant of my son Brian's new militia, turned and acknowledged us with a wave.

We strode over to him, and I introduced Jake. "Jake, this is Chris Rahn, a real U.S. Army First Sergeant. He and my son Brian served in Iraq together. Chris brought us reinforcements from what's left of decent National Guard people."

The two shook hands.

"Iraq, huh?" Jake said. "Who you with?"

"The 10th Mountain," Rahn replied. "You?"

"First Cav, and don't start that 'horse we never rode' crap," Jake replied good-naturedly.

"I would never," Rahn answered.

"You mean the horse they never rode, the bridge they never crossed, and the yellow speaks for

itself? That one?" I asked with what I was sure
was a good imitation of Brian's troublemaker grin.
The saying had to do with the 1st Cavalry Division
patch, which was a large yellow shield containing
a black diagonal slash and a black horse silhouette.

"Yeah, John, that's the one," Jake replied.
"Don't start any shit. I'll show you riding with
my team anytime you want."

"Just teasing, guys, geez. When did the army
get soft?"

"According to my uncle, right after you two
retired from it. It will get soft again when the first
sergeant here retires."

"Well, enough of memory lane," I interrupted.
"Chris, we need to get these guys bunked down,
horses put to pasture, plus store their gear. Jake
don't want to live in the barn come winter, so we'll
need to build two more cabins."

"You building Henryville, John?" Rahn asked,
glancing sideways at me.

I chuckled. "Looks like it, but no. So don't start
that shit, either. Bad enough your prattling on
about the Big House."

"Big house?" Jake asked. "Oh, tell me more,
this could be good."

Taking Jake by the arm, Rahn steered him toward the other soldiers. As they walked away, I

heard him briefly explain. "Well, it's like this, all these small cabins here behind the big cabin…"

*   *   *

One of Brian Henry's soldiers moved the HMMWV under a large elm tree in the middle of a farm field that had been used for hay at one time. The tall grass reached up to about halfway to the top of the thick heavy tires that supported the vehicle.

Two soldiers sat on the ground next to it, their M4 rifles leaning against the body of the vehicle.

Sitting on the hood, his back resting against the windshield, was a young athletically built man in his mid-thirties. He wore ACU pants with tan boots. As was customary for soldiers, he had bloused his pants over the top of his boots. He wore a tan t-shirt and a floppy desert hat that covered the brown hair on his head. Brian Henry searched the distant fields through a pair of binoculars. His elbows resting on his knees as he panned the horizon, periodically stopping to give more attention to anything that he thought warranted it. Right now, it was twin fawns playing just outside of the tree line. He searched for the mother that he knew was nearby.

"See anything, Chief?" one of the soldiers asked. He chewed on the chili macaroni main entre of his MRE, or meals ready to eat. The self-contained heating element, with just a little bit of salt water, had warmed the meal up enough to make it taste good.

"Just a couple of fawns, Travis," Brian Henry responded.

"Doesn't sound too exciting," PFC Chuck Travis said as he dug deeper into the tan pouch of chili mac. "Hopefully, it stays that way; an easy day is a good thing as far as I'm concerned."

"Don't get too used to it. The only easy day was yesterday. At least, that's what the SEALS say," Brian said. "We won't have too many easy ones once we find our target. Shit will get real, and it will get real fast."

"We're gonna have to fight them, aren't we, Chief?" the other soldier asked.

"No doubt about it, Private Roop," Brian answered. He had taken the two youngest, and therefore, greenest soldiers out with him. Being a lead-from-the-front and set-the-example kind of soldier, Brian knew the best way to train these men was to ease them into things without scaring the hell out of them. Teach them the ropes, show them what to do, and, more importantly, why to do it.

"You done eating, Roop?" Brian asked.

"Yes sir," Roop said as he took the packet of candy that were inside the MRE pouch and put them in his uniform blouse pocket.

"Come up here, let me show you something. You, too, Travis," Brian directed.

The two soldiers hopped to their feet, grabbed their weapons, and put the MRE pouches that they had put all of the unused parts back in inside the HMMWV. Moving next to Brian, the two soldiers waited until Brian took the binoculars away from his eyes.

"What do you two know about terrain?" Brian asked.

"Just what they taught me in Basic Training and AIT, sir," Travis answered.

"Same here, sir," was Roop's response. AIT was what the U.S. Army called Advanced Individual Training.

"Well, let me tell you why terrain is your friend and how you can use it to your advantage for both cover and concealment."

For the next 30 odd minutes, Brian explained the different terrain features that were visible to the two young soldiers. He told them how to approach and use tree lines, rises, draws, and gullies to their advantage and to their enemy's disadvantage. Finishing, Brian asked, "You two have any questions?"

They jumped down from their perch. "No, sir," the two men replied together.

"Then, let's get this circus on the road. What did you guys leave me to eat?"

Reaching inside the HMMWV and picking up the one remaining MRE pack, Private Roop said, "Um, well sir, it's chicken pesto pasta."

"Lovely," Brian said. "I shoulda picked first."

"You can have my candy if you want, Chief," Roop offered.

"They make you sterile, Roop, didn't you know that," Brian said as he hid his grin.

"Oh shit, I mean… No sir, I didn't…"

"Get in the Hummer, Roop, and take the SAW. Travis, you drive."

"Yes, sir," the two men replied.

The trio got inside the vehicle, 'mounted' as Brian called it, and slowly drove across the field toward the far tree line.

After navigating through a down fence and the wayward strands of barbed wire, Travis drove the HMMWV onto the road where it slowly began its journey south toward the old Department of Natural Resources Fishery.

*   *   *

The black FEMA HMMWV drove steadily on the paved road not far from the fishery, where the biker gang had set up. Now abandoned by them, there was no chance of seeing anyone else on the road unless they were the target that the FEMA men were seeking.

The slow speed of the vehicle, the warm day, and the steady hum of the tires on the blacktop lulled the two men inside into a lethargic state. As the driver tried to pay attention to the road ahead, his passenger alternated between nodding asleep and watching the world go by out of the side window.

"You awake over there?" the driver asked.

"Yeah, I'm awake. It isn't easy, though. This is some boring shit," the passenger replied. "Reminds me of when I was a kid in Kansas sitting in the back seat of my dad's car watching farm fields out the window. The scenery is prettier here, but it's farm fields and woods, farm fields and woods."

"I know. I keep nodding off. Driving is all that is keeping me awake. Wish we could open these windows."

"Yeah, open windows would be nice. We should pull off soon, my bladder's getting full."

"The map says the fishery is around here. Think they have any fish?" the driver remarked.

"Maybe. We could grab some and take them back to the armory. Beats MREs," the passenger said.

"Oh yeah, all fileted and packaged just waiting for us. I grew up in Michigan and we had a lot of fisheries there. Mostly minnows and very small fish, fingerlings I think they called them, which they'd dump in the rivers and lakes to hopefully grow up into bigger fish. That's all the fish you'll find there if they even lived through the EMP."

"You gonna pull over or what? I gotta go. My back teeth are starting to float."

The driver pulled the HMMWV over to the side of the road, stopping the vehicle. He turned off the engine and said, "Here ya' go, TB."

"TB?"

"Yeah, TB—tiny bladder. Geez, we stopped not half an hour ago so you could pee. If I was my dad, I'd tell ya' to hold it till we stopped to get gas."

"Mine was the same way," the passenger remarked as he stepped out of the vehicle and walked to the side of the road. He undid his pants and proceeded to relieve himself.

The driver exited his door and stretched. Deciding to walk around, he turned toward an opening in the woods that appeared to lead toward a field. The hum of insects was loud in his ear, and he waved his hand, swatting them away.

"Where are you going?" the passenger shouted.

"Just over here. There's a trail here, looks like a road. I want to see where it goes," he shouted back.

"Okay, don't go far. We aren't supposed to leave the vehicles and go exploring."

The words no sooner left the passenger's mouth than a loud roar and squeal shattered the silence.

"What the fuck!" the driver exclaimed.

*   *   *

"What the fuck!" PFC Travis shouted as he rounded the curve in the road, then slammed on the brakes of the Hummer.

Private Roop lurched forward in the turret, grabbing the SAW for support.

Brian quickly threw his hands up toward the windshield, stopping himself and hearing a loud snap. In front of them was a black FEMA HMMWV. Two occupants were outside of the vehicle, one standing in the ditch on the passenger side and the other in the middle of the road. Neither man was armed, but both began to run toward their HMMWV.

"FIRE 'EM UP, ROOP!" Brian shouted.

The young soldier, too scared to do anything but obey, grabbed the SAW and pulled the trigger.

A stream of 5.56 mm rounds flew toward the black HMMWV, piercing the hood and spiderwebbing the front windshield. It also had the effect of stopping the two black-clad FEMA soldiers in their tracks.

The two men stood there, fully exposed as Roop traversed the SAW first toward one and then the other. In a display of youthful bravado, Roop ordered, "Put your hands up! Put your hands on your head, interlock your fingers and get on your knees."

First one and then the other obeyed, raising their hands skyward. The two men shared a glance but didn't move.

Roop put another short burst of 5.56 from the SAW into the HMMWV. "NOW, GODDAM-MIT!" he shouted.

The men followed his instructions as Travis exited the vehicle, his M4 pointed at the man in the road. "Keep the SAW on the other one, Bill," Travis yelled.

Brian exited the vehicle from his side, cradling his left arm. The grimace on his face suggested a significant amount of pain. Taking his shemagh from his pocket, the one he'd carried since his first tour in Iraq, he used his teeth and right hand to tie a knot. Draping it over his neck, he used it as a sling. "Roop, that son of a bitch so much as scratches, you light him up," Brian ordered.

"Yes, Chief."

"You okay, Chief?" Travis asked.

"I'll be fine, just keep an eye on your boy there. If he does anything you don't like, shoot his ass."

"Yes, Chief."

Brain went over to the HMMWV and looked inside. He found two MP4s, two patrol packs similar to the Army 3-day assault pack, but in black instead of the Army Combat Uniform pattern. There were also maps, and of course, several MREs.

You'd think these clowns would have regular food instead of this crap.

Pulling each pack out one at a time, Brian left the MREs and then took the map and map case that was in the front of the vehicle. Pointing at the FEMA soldier on the side of the road, Brian yelled, "You!" and then wiggled his fingers, indicating he wanted the man to come to him.

As the man started to stand, he dropped his hands. A three-round burst from the SAW made everyone jump as Roop did what he was told.

"Hands in the air, asshole," Roop yelled, and the FEMA soldier immediately complied.

"Now, on your feet," Roop ordered.

"I need my hands to push myself up," the FEMA man replied.

"Walk on your knees toward the front of the vehicle. I want to see all of you."

The FEMA soldier, in an over-exaggerated manner, walked on his knees toward the front of the black HMMWV until he was fully exposed.

"Now, you can use your hands. Put 'em right back up there when you are standing."

The man quickly complied and now stood with his hands on his head.

Brian, trying hard to suppress the grin at Roop's efforts, went to the man and using his one good hand and arm unzipped the plate carrier vest the man was wearing. The vest had multiple pockets with spare magazines for the MP4s that were found inside the HMMWV, an M9 sidearm, and extra magazines for it, too.

Taking his handgun out of the leg holster he carried it in, Brian pressed the pistol against the man's head. "Slowly drop your arms and let this carrier fall off of you. Make a wrong move and it's lights out. Got it?"

The FEMA soldier shook his head up and down and dropped his arms as ordered. He had to shrug his shoulders a couple of times to get it to fall off completely.

"Now, step away, get on your knees, and cross your ankles," Brian told him.

The man quickly followed directions.

Brian then went to the man in the road and went through the same process with him. Finishing he said, "Travis, get some of those zip cuffs out of the back and cuff these two clowns. They have some 'splainin to do."

"Hooah, Chief." Travis led the two men to the side of the road where they sat in the shade provided by their HMMWV. Roop had come out of the turret and stood guard over the two men as Travis tried to assist with Brian's arm.

"Chief, I'm sorry. They were just there all of a sudden," he explained.

Travis put a short splint on Brian's arm that immobilized his wrist. As he wrapped the arm with an ace wrap from the HMMWV's first aid kit, he continued to apologize.

"Enough Travis, shit happens. It's not like you did this on purpose, or did you?" Brian joked.

"Oh no, Chief, no. I'd never do that," Travis replied.

Brian quickly realized the young soldier was not getting the joke. "It's okay, Travis. It was an accident."

Brian could tell he was still troubled. "Go relieve Roop. I need to talk with him," Brian said gently.

"Chief, I'm so…"

"It's okay, Travis. It was an accident. I'll heal just fine," Brian interrupted.

"Yes, sir." The young soldier picked up his weapon and went over to Roop to guard the two FEMA soldiers.

Roop returned and stood in front of Brian. "You wanted to see me, Chief?"

"Yes, PFC Roop," Brian replied.

"Sir, I'm a PV2."

"You're wrong, PFC Roop. You are now a Private First Class. You did real good and reacted quickly. I'm proud of you."

"Gee, Sir, thank you."

"So tell me, where did you learn to sound off like a bull moose? I think you scared those two FEMA boys more by yelling than you did with the SAW."

"I don't know, Chief. It just sorta came out."

"Well, it most certainly came out. If I may, though, perhaps next time a little less enthusiasm.

You don't want to distract your patrol mates as they wonder who the man with the big voice is."

"Yes, sir. I'll remember that," Roop said, standing a little taller.

"Let's go talk to our guests, shall we? We need to figure out what to do with them."

"You want me to shoot 'em, Chief?" Roop asked.

With a slight chuckle, Brian said, "Not yet, Roop. Maybe later. Now grab the radio out of the Hummer and then join me and Travis. We need to find out what these boys have to say."

CHAPTER 3

"The best revenge is not to be like your enemy."

—Marcus Aurelius

We got Jake and his people settled in. Wasn't that much to it as all we had to do was put the horses in the corral, show them where they would bunk until we got cabins made for them, and then get them introduced to the soldiers we had here.

We had three patrols out, taking up all but one of our HMMWVs. I was concerned with not sending out the three Hummers with SAW mounts but also wary if we had to react quickly, we'd need a SAW for whatever we might face. It was decided that we'd hold Johnson's vehicle in reserve. He said it was his and Rahn chose not to argue with him.

We had two-man teams out in all vehicles except for the one Brian took. He'd decided to take our youngest two soldiers out with him. He and Rahn argued for twenty minutes over that. Brian eventually wore him down, or Rahn just quit.

Jake, Rahn, Craig, and I had been in the barn discussing how we might use the horse patrols and turn them into a definite advantage. Their ability to go places the HMMWVs couldn't, as well as other mobility issues, was an advantage we couldn't turn down.

I was starting to feel good about our chances when I heard a voice shouting my name.

"JOHN, John!" the woman's voice shouted.

I went to the doorway of the barn and saw Linda running towards us. "John, they've had contact," she said, breathing hard from the run.

"Contact?" I asked. "Who had contact?"

"Brian and his team. They ran into a FEMA Team," she explained, still trying to catch her breath.

"What happened?"

"Well, give me a minute, dammit," she said sharply.

Taking a deep breath, she explained. "Brian called on the radio. They ran into a FEMA team near the fish hatchery. They captured two men, questioned them, and then Brian sent them walking. They are bringing the FEMA Hummer. He called it a Hummer." She had a devilish grin on her face when she said that. I wasn't touching that comment with a 10-foot pole. "He said they were towing it back, that he couldn't leave it for the bad guys. He actually called them 'bad guys'. He also said he thinks he broke his arm."

"Broke his arm?" Craig remarked. "What the hell was he doing that he broke his arm?"

"He didn't say," Linda answered. "He told me to find you, John, and tell you. Said they'd be here in about half an hour."

"Okay, thank you," I said as Rahn and I exchanged looks.

"If our first blood in this is a simple broken arm, we came out good," Rahn said. "I wonder what the rest of the story is?"

"We'll find out when he gets here. Did he say anything else, Linda?" I asked.

"That was the message, so you know what I know," she answered. "I have work to do," she added, and then went back to the cabin.

"Good-looking woman," Jake said.

"She's spoken for," Rahn said.

"Knock it off, Chris," I told him firmly. "That stuff is going to get out of hand."

"Hey, I'm not interested. Nothing to worry about from me. I just appreciate real beauty," Jake said.

"We need to get ready for Brian when he returns. We should recall the other patrols, too," I suggested.

"I'll let Sam know to sound the recall," Craig said as he headed toward the barn where Sam had his Ham radio in the loft.

We'd intended to set him up in his cabin that he shared with Gary and Rick. Sam liked the barn loft better and the height of the barn allowed his antenna to be placed much higher as well. As long as he was happy with the location, I didn't care.

"Let's wait for him on the porch," I said.

*   *   *

"How many patrols do we have out today that have called in," Wolfe asked. He and Captain Roy Jamison were enjoying a mid-day cup of coffee as they stood in the Communications room of the armory. They had several teams out, each with a different sector and each with the same mission—to find the Henry compound.

"All but one," Jamison replied. Raising the cup of coffee, he held it to his lips and sipped. Pausing as he savored the taste, he lowered the cup, went to a green military folding field table that was against the wall, and grabbed two packets of sugar. He added those to his coffee, removed a pen from his pocket, and used it to stir the coffee. "I'm going to have to remind these people what it means when I say *check in every hour*."

"Maybe they are in a bad spot, sir," a radio operator said. He was part of a team that had arrived yesterday from Wausau that augmented the first Quick Reaction Force team. The arrival of a few radio operators and ten more shooters, as well as four vehicles, was a much-needed addition to the QRF Team.

"Maybe. Maybe they're jerking off out there, too," Jamison said somewhat absently. Making eye contact with Wolfe, he signaled they should leave the room.

Exiting, the two men headed down the long hall.

"Let's go to my office, Elias," Jamison said.

Like the compliant person he had become, Wolfe followed the FEMA leader down the hall to what had once been Wolfe's personal office. Much had changed in the last few months.

"Close the door," Jamison said as they entered his office. "I hope we didn't have another ambush of my men out there. These Henrys are getting under my skin."

"Want me to see what I can find?" Wolfe asked.

"You do want to get out there, don't you," Jamison said, a bit of snark in his tone. "What's your motivation, Elias? Why do you want out there so bad?"

"I'm a soldier and I..." he began.

"Oh, bullshit. If I hear another because I'm a soldier speech from one of you National Guard types, I'm gonna vomit." Softening his tone, he asked, "So what is it?"

"Rahn," he replied.

"Rahn, the first sergeant?"

"Yup. I had a good thing going with Barstow. Rahn's betrayal made me look bad," Wolfe explained.

Jamison laughed. "You had a good thing going because that's what Barstow *wanted* you to think. He needed your soldiers to do his dirty work. There weren't enough of us. Rahn actually hurt him, not you. He doesn't give two shits about you," he exclaimed. "You're a fucking pawn, Wolfe. Just like me. The difference is you're more expendable."

Raising his voice, Wolfe asked, "Does it matter? Does it really matter if we are being used? Hell, the army used me, so what's the difference? I'll tell you. The difference is, we're on top of the food chain right now and Rahn almost messed that up.

He and the Henrys, and whoever else they have out there, are in our way. We have to exterminate them. We have to destroy what they are doing because if we don't, it will be us dancing on the end of a rope. I know where I want to be." Wiping his mouth, Wolfe stood defiantly in front of Jamison, glaring at the man.

"You surprise me," Jamison said with almost no emotion. "I figured you for a pussy and not an opportunist. I like what I see."

"Then, let's destroy those assholes together. We have to find them and end them. Every last one. No prisoners, no survivors," Wolfe said.

"Go hunting, Elias. Take two men and one of the Hummers and go hunting."

Hearing those words, Wolfe turned and left the room.

Exiting the building, he shouted, "I need two men and a vehicle. We're going hunting!"

*   *   *

I could hear the rattle of the field phone from the porch. Jake, Rahn, and I hadn't said much once we got there. Each lost in our own thoughts, we chatted nonsensically for a few minutes and then we went quiet. Craig joined us and said Sam had recalled all of the patrols. Everyone would be in soon.

"I think once they're all back, we need to plan how we will use Jake's people and our people together to patrol, or whatever it is we have them do," Rahn said seriously.

"I agree, but we need to start thinking of ourselves as *us* instead of Jake and us. We are all in this together now," I said.

Donna and Linda came out on the porch. As always, with the squeak of the spring announcing the door was opening.

"They're here," Donna said, as she and Linda, medical bags in hand, started to walk toward the driveway where we could see the vehicles arriving—the desert camouflaged HMMWV pulling the flat black one. Inside the black HMMWV, Brian sat in the driver's seat.

I could see one soldier in the turret and the other driving our vehicle. As they came to a stop, the black vehicle rolled a bit longer, then stopped.

Brian struggled with the door, but he got it open and exited with a grunt. I saw his left forearm splinted to the hand and in a sling.

Donna jogged over to him, Linda right behind her as they made him sit on the ground. I chuckled at what I imagined the conversation between them was Brian saying he was fine, Donna saying he needed to be examined, and so on. Donna would win, but the debate was entertaining, regardless.

Rahn was already up and heading for the two soldiers. Both had dismounted from the vehicle and were waiting for him.

"Travis, Roop," Rahn said. "Want to give me an after-action report? We'll start with how Chief hurt himself."

"Yes, First Sergeant. I was driving and had to slam on the brakes when we came upon the FEMA vehicle and crew. Chief stuck his hand up to stop himself and it hit the windshield. He said he heard a crack, so we're guessing it's broke," Travis explained.

"I was in the turret, First Sergeant," Roop added. "I almost fell out when Travis hit the brakes."

"Roop did good, First Sergeant. He stitched that vehicle right up with the SAW. Scared the shit out of the two FEMA boys," Travis said.

"Chief promoted me to PFC, First Sergeant," Roop said with a giant grin.

"Oh, he did," Rahn said, finally getting a word in.

"Yes, First Sergeant," the two soldiers said together.

"Pull this black piece of junk over to the barn and then go get cleaned up. We'll talk more in a bit. Good job, you two," Rahn ordered.

"You betchya, First Sergeant," the happy young soldiers replied. Travis got back in the HMMWV and Roop went to the FEMA vehicle.

"They look pleased," I said as I approached Rahn. "Let's see how our wounded warrior is doing."

"Yeah, they did well. Seems Brian wasn't wearing a seat belt and stopped himself with his hand on the windshield," he replied as we walked up on Brian.

"How're you doing?" I asked.

"It looks like a minor fracture of his wrist," Donna said as she finished rewrapping it.

"Will he live?" I asked.

"Oh yeah, it's a long way from his heart. There are no bones sticking out, and he's still a smart ass," she answered.

"Hey, I'm sitting right here, have pity on me. I'm wounded," Brian piped in.

"Donna says you'll live, so stop whining," I said.

Rahn stood there grinning. "You promoted Roop?"

"Yep, he did good. The boy's a regular Rambo. He has a voice on him like a bullhorn, terrified the two FEMA guys," Brian said.

"What did you do with them?" Rahn asked.

Brian looked up at Rahn. "I think Roop wanted to shoot 'em. We interrogated them. I have a lot of information on Wolfe, they were so scared they didn't know when to shut up. Then, I sent them back toward Antigo."

"That's gonna go over well. I wonder how long before Wolfe radios me with another threat," I joined in.

Brian glanced at me. "He's not in charge. Some FEMA captain named Jamison is."

"Roy Jamison, Commander of the FEMA QRF," Rahn injected. "A real hard ass. I saw him execute a prisoner once for allegedly stealing food."

"They're located in the old armory in Antigo. They have, according to the two men we questioned, over thirty people. Might be an exaggeration, though," Brian added.

"Might not be. His team had twenty-five-ish in it, and they probably brought extras," Rahn said, giving Brian a sideways glance.

"They don't know where we are, either, but they are looking—and looking hard," said Brian. "They told us they had a half dozen patrols out looking for us. We only saw this one, and now they're down a vehicle."

"Two, when you count the one from the other day. They aren't going to be happy about that. We need to step up the patrols, and now that Jake Kook is here with nine others, plus two horses each, we're looking pretty good for doing just that," I said.

"So, we've got over thirty military effectives," Rahn tallied.

"Thirty-four by my count," Brian interjected.

"Slightly less than that," I said. "Two of those, Nancy and Linda, aren't going out and will stay here. Sam is going to have to stay on the radio, and we should leave Donna back here, too. She and Linda are our only medical support. Gary, too. He talks a tough game, but his knees and back have been giving him hell. Rahn's right, about thirty effectives."

"Couple of my guys are good with battlefield first aid, John," Rahn added. "But I hear ya'. Thirty effectives."

"We also have area knowledge; they don't know where we are, they don't know what we have, and we have surprise on our side," Brian said. "It'll be close, but we got this. Old combat rules say to attack someplace you have to have with at least twice as many as the defenders."

"That's really old, son. With modern weapons, that ratio goes way down. But you're right. We have all of those other things going for us. Once these ladies get done with you, we need to have a strategy session with you, Rahn, and Jake. Time to step up our patrols, and we need to talk to the Winstons, too. They won't come here, but they are exposed out there and aren't as secluded as we are," I said.

"Oh, I think he's fixed up, John," Donna said. "Whoever splinted him up did a good job, and it's probably just a hairline or simple break. Can't really tell without x-rays, but he should be fine. At least, we don't have to try an amputation."

"Amputation!" Brian exclaimed. "Seriously?"

"Not yet," Donna said. "If it gets infected, we will," she added as she winked at me.

"Seriously?" Brian said again.

"Yes, seriously, you klutz," Nancy said as she approached the group and rushed toward Brian. "I see you once again managed to hurt yourself. FIL told me they used to call you Band-aid Brian. Are we going to have to resurrect that name?"

"It wasn't my fault, Nancy," Brian exclaimed. He opened up his good arm and tried to hug her.

"You poor baby," Nancy mused, giving him the hug he was after.

"Let's go to the porch. Thanks, ladies. If I didn't say it before, I will now. I'm glad you're here. I don't know what we'd do without you," I said as I turned and headed back to my chair.

"You ain't amputating anything, Donna," Brian yelled as I walked away.

Rahn was next to me, chuckling. "That should slow him down for a day or two."

*   *   *

Wolfe and his two-man team raced down the highway, pushing the limits of the HMMWV. As they drove through Elton, Wolfe looked at the map. The county road to take to Lake View was just up ahead and he ordered the driver to slow down so they could make the turn.

A few miles down the county road, Wolfe saw two men walking toward them. Both dressed in black. "Shit," he muttered. "Pull over, driver. Let's pick up our men."

The driver pulled to the side of the road, and Wolfe sat there, waiting for the two men on foot to reach them.

No way we're going to drive up to meet them. They obviously lost their vehicle. I should make them walk all the way back.

When the two men were close enough, Wolfe got out and said, "What happened?"

"We were ambushed, sir. They shot up our vehicle."

"You don't look too worse for the wear. Where are your weapons?" Wolfe asked.

"They took them, sir. Gave us these MREs and said to start walking."

Wolfe stared hard, frustrated at them. "Get in the vehicle. Show me where this happened."

"Yes, sir. It's a few miles down the road, by the fish hatchery."

"Go, driver," Wolfe ordered.

The driver sped off, spinning the tires on the loose gravel of the roadside.

A few moments later, one of the men said, "Right here, sir."

They could see the turn off for the hatchery ahead, but nothing more.

"Show me what happened," Wolfe ordered as he exited the HMMWV.

The two men got out as well as one of the other FEMA men. The driver stayed with the vehicle.

They walked Wolfe through what happened. A few spent brass shell casings were on the road—all that remained of the ambush the soldiers had described.

Wolfe glared at them. "They took your vehicle? I thought you said your vehicle was shot up. Where is it?"

The man nodded. "I saw them towing it away, sir. They took it."

"Well, just how many men ambushed you?" Wolfe asked.

"There was three, and they had an automatic weapon, a SAW."

"Did you even shoot back? Did you defend yourself?"

The other man shook his head. "They were on us before we knew it."

"I've seen enough. Get in the vehicle," Wolfe ordered, disgust obvious in his tone.

After everyone was inside, the driver asked, "Where to, sir?"

"Back to the armory."

CHAPTER 4

*"Let me not pray to be sheltered from dangers,
but to be fearless in facing them."*

—Rabindranath Tagore

Jake, Brian, Rahn, and I sat in a circle of chairs on the porch. Things were starting to get serious, and we knew that FEMA was going to keep probing our area until they found us. The event near the hatchery confirmed they were looking for us. Our greatest concern was in keeping them away for as long as possible. We could not allow them to find where we lived. The thought of putting everyone at risk coupled with winter wasn't that far away and our survivability if we were run out—the problems just kept getting bigger.

"The way I see things, we have two objectives for these patrols. One is obvious; we need to know what FEMA is up to and when they are in our area. The other is to use the horse mounted scouts and our vehicle patrols much like our ancestors used cavalry; as a screening force to keep them away," I began.

"Speak for yourself, John," Jake remarked.

Brian high-fived him, so I now knew those two had bonded. Their sense of humor could be a good thing as time went on. It would help keep up morale. It could also be a detriment if people got carried away with it, and I wasn't talking about them. We had a large number of younger men in our force, and young men could easily get caught up in things. I didn't need clowning and grab-assing run amok. For now, I chose to ignore it.

"We can keep sending out the HMMWV patrols as we have. What we need to figure out is how best to use Jakes's people to scout, and where necessary, to harass FEMA," I said. "Brian, what did you learn about the capabilities of our esteemed enemy?"

"Well, as I shared when I was being threatened with an amputation, there are about thirty of them, maybe more, maybe less. They have more than likely as many vehicles as we do. They don't appear to have any automatic weapons outside of the automatic mode of their M4s. The FEMA troops don't impress me too much from a combat training standpoint because both times we've engaged them they failed miserably," he explained.

"You said they'd moved into the armory in Antigo?" Rahn asked.

"Yes, one of them told me they had moved into the armory. They also took a couple of locals as servants. They are doing the cleaning, cooking, that kind of stuff," he answered.

"Let me share my experience with regard to their combat capabilities," Rahn said. "These are not combat soldiers, but they *can* be ruthless. For the most part, they are security at the camps in Wausau. The QRF is designed to put down riots and other prisoner uprisings. They have shot unarmed people, tortured them, and according to a couple of my soldiers—our soldiers, Chief—they have abused female prisoners."

"You talking rape, Chris?" I asked.

"Yes, they can be especially crude, if rape isn't crude enough. Specialist Hart caught a couple of them. He almost killed them with his bare hands and an ax handle that was nearby. He had to be restrained. It took everything I could to keep him out of the stockade, or worse," he answered.

The porch went silent. The reality of Rahn's words sunk in deeply and disturbed us all.

"Okay," I said, breaking the silence. "Jake, tell me how you think it best we use your people."

"We are good at stealth," Jake said, looking at me. "Several of my guys are veterans. Marines, so don't be hatin,' army guys. Our range is limited on horseback, but at the same time, it's easier for us to hide. We can stay out overnight, shoot and scoot if necessary, and provide that shield you were talking about, John."

"I'm a bit concerned with overnight," Brian piped in. "However, with their stealth ability, I like that. Stealth horses. With their stealth ability, they do have the ability to RON and be a more effective scout and screening force."

"RON? Is that an army word?" Jake asked.

"Sorry, no. RON, Remain Over Night. It's an aviator's term. They use it when due to a long flight, they need to rest up before returning to base. So they spend the night where they are. Same thing here, only it's a long ride," Brian replied. "Communication is my biggest worry. How many radios do we have and what is their range, Dad?"

"I've got six BaoFeng UV-82HP high power dual band radios in the basement with a range of anywhere from 2 miles to 15 miles. I also have spare batteries. The HMMWV patrols can use their SINCGARS just as they have been.

Everything will integrate with Sam's Ham," I explained.

"Guys, really, c'mon. Sam's Ham, what is this Doctor Suess? And what the hell is a sinkcigar?" Jake asked.

"Marines," Brian said, shaking his head.

"I was army. Some of my guys were marines, but I was a clerk. We didn't use radios," Jake said. "I still don't know what a sinkcigar is."

"SINCGARS is a Single Channel Ground and Airborne Radio System," Rahn explained. "It integrates with both land and air communications and is satellite capable. We won't be using the satellite part. And before you ask, Sam's Ham is Sam Karpinski's Ham radio that's up in the loft of the barn. Sam is our ears to the world. That's how we knew that, for the most part, we were on our own. That's also how we know more bad shit can be coming this way, so pray for an early winter to slow it down."

"Welcome to the apocalypse," Jake said to no one in particular.

"Pretty much," I said. "So, we have communications mostly solved. We just need a plan for how these scout teams will go out. I don't want any lone wolfing it out there. All teams have two people, even yours, Jake. They'll need that to keep alert, and in case communications go down, they'll need to send someone back. Ideas?"

It was quiet for a moment. I assumed everyone was thinking. After almost two minutes, or what seemed that long, Brian said, "What I suggest is that Jake, Rahn, and I get together with our maps and come up with a plan. We're doing the operation, Dad, so no offense, but let us plan it."

"Sounds fine with me," I said, hoping I didn't sound surprised or stunned. I actually agreed with him. They knew their people better than I did, and they were going to be conducting the mission, so let *them* plan it.

"We'll get back to you as soon as we put something together. You can pick it apart or whatever you feel the need to do," Brian said.

I took that last part as a bit of snark, but Brian had been asserting his leadership for a while now. I figured he was telling me he knew what he was doing. I guess I was falling into the role of patriarch, but that wasn't happening. I wasn't ready to sit here on the porch and wave at the parade going by.

*   *   *

As Wolfe finished explaining to Captain Jamison what the two men had told him about how they'd lost their vehicle, the look on Jamison's face sent a powerful message. He was not happy. "I should have those two cowards horsewhipped," he almost shouted, and then, taking a deep breath, he managed to calm himself. "For now, we need them, but I'm getting on the radio with Barstow and asking for more people. It might be time to bring up some of your troops."

"They'll do the job, but we better hand-select them," Wolfe said, giving Jamison a pointed but questioning look. "I don't want to bring up any closet Rahn supporters, and I'm sure there are some back there."

"You should pick them. I need you back here in 48 hours, though. This shit needs to stop."

"Yes, it does, but we don't even know where they are. We can't fight 'em if we can't find 'em."

"Oh, we'll find them, Elias. I'll increase the size and number of patrols. We'll start harassing the few people in town instead of bringing them here. Make their lives miserable, so to speak. We'll find them," Jamison said with a chilling voice. "I want you back here with as many men as you can vett, bring extra ammunition and automatic weapons. I should've thought of that to begin with."

"I'll leave now and be back in two days, Roy," Elias said. His use of Jamison's first name was not lost on the captain.

Grabbing his hat, Wolfe shifted his leg holster for his sidearm, put the hat on his head, and headed out the door.

Now, I've got patrols to engage. A little war is hell on the civilian population, Jamison thought as he followed Wolfe through the door and down the hall. It was time for him to engage a couple of teams in FEMA terrorism, and he knew just the team.

Arriving at the vehicle assembly area, Jamison saw four young men sitting on one of the vehicles. "You men look bored. Want some excitement in your lives?"

"Hell yeah, Captain, anything is better than sitting around here or driving through the countryside looking at cows," one of the men replied.

"Any of you part of that team that grabbed the turkeys from those backwoods hicks?" Jamison asked.

"I was, Captain," another man replied.

"Do you think you can go back out there and find where they live?"

"Yes, sir. You want us to burn them out?"

Jamison shook his head. "No, I want you to find where they live. Then, I want you to come back here and tell me."

"Yes, sir," the man replied.

"Head out tomorrow morning, early. It's too late in the day to go searching anymore. Find their home, don't do anything else, and come back here ASAP."

"Yes, sir, we can do that." The man nodded.

"Good, entertainment will begin afterward. I think you men will enjoy the plan I'm putting together," Jamison said.

As he walked away, Jamison heard one of the men say, "It sounds like we're finally going to have some fun around here. It's been boring ever since we got here, and there ain't no women around, if you know what I mean."

Jamison grinned.

*   *   *

Brian and his new crew headed off for the barn; I sat quietly on the porch. I hated sitting quietly anywhere, especially now. It made me feel uncomfortable and I didn't like being uncomfortable. However, I must've jinxed myself because the screen door squeaked and out trooped the ladies.

I was surprised all four of them were together. Usually, one of them was in the bunker or out back on watch. Obviously, that was not the case tonight.

I mustered up some courage and said, "Yes, ladies, how can I be of assistance?" I could tell by the four sets of eyes glaring at me that I chose unwisely.

"John Henry, we need to talk," Donna said.

There goes her using my full name again, but this time, I think I'm in trouble. Flashbacks to my mother saying my name went racing through my head, and I prepared myself for the worst.

"Okay," I said, "what would you like to talk about?" I swallowed a bit hard at this point.

"We are not just cooks, nurses, and caregivers, John Henry." This time it was Nancy and I was seeing her ABW in full force. "Me and Addie have both fought against people who wanted to hurt us, and I was injured. But we survived. We aren't fragile little things you men have to keep in the house and protect all the time."

"So, what are you asking?" I said, meeting her eyes.

"We demand the equal right to do what the men are doing. Patrols, fighting if it comes to it. You know damn good and well what we are asking," Nancy explained.

"She's right, John, and you know she is," Donna added. "You can't keep us wrapped up in here when you need everyone to help out."

"That's right, *JOHN*," Nancy interrupted.

The way she pronounced my name made me shudder. Plus, she usually called me FIL. These ladies were *angry*.

"We can do more than house chores. You'll need all of us to help with what's coming. We're all exposed here, not just the boys."

I respected Nancy's opinion. She had been wounded and stepped up when we needed her. She also showed her mettle when the gang banger/biker, whatever he was, showed up for Mike.

"You're right," I said.

The silence was deafening.

The four women stood there, staring. Eventually, a shuffle of feet came, them shifting from one foot to the other and arms crossed and uncrossed.

Nancy spoke first. "We're right? That's it?"

Donna, the only other woman who really knew me intimately had that "what are you up to, John" look on her face.

"I said you're right. You ladies are not domestic servants. You aren't here to run the household, and you've shown that. I have no excuse." While I was laying it on kind of thick, I knew they were right. Not only would we need them, but I *had been* sheltering them from much of what was going on. I didn't even realize I was doing it.

"So when do we start?" Donna asked.

"Brian, Rahn, and Jake are making patrol plans now. When they have a plan, we'll talk to them and get you into the rotation. Something we *do* need to think about, Donna, is who is our medical team. Right now, that's you and Linda. Your skills are incomparable. You need to think about your role in all of this and how you fit in. If you're running around the countryside shooting up FEMA, then you aren't here taking care of our wounded if we need you two here for that."

"You have a point," she said.

Linda had been quiet and still not said a word. Nor had Addie, except for when the conversation had first started.

"Linda, what do you think? How do your medical skills compare to Donna's?" I asked.

Linda gave me a thoughtful look. "She's a nurse, John. Her skills are way beyond mine. I know drugs, herbs, and how to make concoctions from them."

"And those are skills I don't have," Donna quickly interjected. "She can also suture, set a bone, and do splints."

"So what happens when the two of you are out there," I used my head to indicate the surrounding woods, "and we need you here? This isn't about being a girl. It's about skill. And trust me, if we need you to pick up a weapon and get into the fight, then the shit has hit the proverbial fan. It will not be pretty if that happens."

"Linda and I will put our heads together and figure it out. We'll let you know," Donna said.

"Rahn may have input as well. He has a few men with some medical training. I'll talk to him."

"When will Brian and the others be done planning?" Nancy asked. She still had that severe tone in her voice and it came through now as she asked the question.

"I don't know. Honestly, ladies, we don't have a lot of time, so I expect they'll be back soon."

"Let us know, then. We want to be involved," Nancy replied.

The four women walked inside the cabin and I heard quiet chatter.

Linda had looked at me out of the corner of her eye, so I wondered what that was about. We had just survived an ambush, and I was tired from the stress of worrying about everyone and everything. Maybe I should think about delegating more; we certainly had the skills in our little band.

If I hadn't been getting low, I would've had a cigar. I'd have to talk with Jake about trying to find a source. I was pretty sure I'd heard him say there were tobacco farms on the Rez.

*   *   *

Jamison woke early. As he sat on the edge of his cot, he thought about the team he was sending out.

"What the hell, why not?" he said aloud.

Getting dressed, he put on his leg holster and grabbed his M4. *I'm going with them.*

The men were just finishing loading what they thought they'd need for their mission. As Jamison strode up to them, one of the men nudged another with his elbow and, pointing with his chin, indicated Jamison approaching.

"Mornin', Captain," the man said.

"Mornin'," said Jamison. "I thought I'd join you on your little excursion today."

"Wanna get on the fun, is that it, Captain?" one of the men asked.

"I didn't come up here to sit in an office and let you boys take all the risks," he replied. "You have everything you need?"

"Yes, sir, we do. Brought extra ammo and magazines, too. Even have a box of flex cuffs."

"You won't need the flex cuffs today," Jamison replied icily. "We won't be bringing anyone back with us."

"Yes, sir," the man said. The look on his face showed worry. Either way, he was all in for the mission. "You want to ride with me, Captain Jamison?"

"Sure, that will work," Jamison replied.

Jamison entered the front passenger seat in the black HMMWV as the two other FEMA troops entered the back seat. The second HMMWV had a driver, plus three passengers inside, with another man riding in the cargo bed in the rear.

The sun was starting to peek on the eastern horizon as they drove out of the armory compound, heading east toward Lake View and their quarry.

"What's your name?" Jamison asked the driver.

"Edmiston, sir," he replied.

"Edmiston, do you know where you are going?"

"I have a good idea, Captain." The man nodded, keeping his eyes on the road. "I saw the direction they rode off in, and based on what they said, I have a good sense of where they live. Shouldn't take us more than an hour to find them."

"Then, let's speed this train up, shall we. I want to catch them at breakfast."

Edmiston pressed his right foot down on the accelerator, propelling the HMMWV forward with a jerk. "YES, SIR!" he said enthusiastically.

It didn't take long for Edmiston to find where they had confronted the Winston brothers.

"It was right about here, sir," Edmiston said. "They rode down the road that way and then turned off. I'd bet they live less than a mile from here, two at most."

"Stop the vehicle. Get the other men assembled. I want to explain how this will go down."

"Yes, sir," Edmiston replied.

CHAPTER 5

*"Good can exist without evil,
whereas evil cannot exist without good."*

—Thomas Aquinas

Charlie Winston had awakened that morning extra early. While it was his custom to get up with the sun, today he was up well before it. Born to the farm.

The Winston family were what was locally known as "Kentucks." Backwoods people from Kentucky who had immigrated to the Northwoods over the years. Hard scrabble and independent people, they lived a simple life with little in the way of modern conveniences. They were self-dependent and rarely asked for help from outsiders. If they couldn't make it or fix it, they figured they didn't need it.

The Winstons were farmers and had a small cornfield and hogs. The barn held a few horses and a rusty but working tractor. Their farmhouse was unpainted and the yard strewn with equipment and a trailer. The refuse and detritus common to people like them.

Getting out of bed, Charlie pulled on his tan overalls covering the sweat-stained and once white long-sleeved t-shirt. He slipped on his boots—he slept with his socks on and had done so as long as he could remember—and grabbed his green farm cap. Then, he headed out through the bedroom door.

A voice behind him stopped him in his tracks.

"You're up early," a sleepy woman's voice said.

Lucille Winston, the love of his life, had married Charlie almost fifty years ago. She was still as pretty as the day he met her.

He winked at her. "I just woke up. No sense layin' around in bed," he replied. "Work to do."

"Was a time you and I used to do a lot of laying around," she said, rolling over, pulling the blanket up over her.

"Yup," he replied, "was a time. No time for that today."

Then, softening his departure, he went to her side of the bed and leaned over to kiss her forehead. "I love you, Lucy. Go back to sleep now."

Walking down the stairs, he stopped at the gun cabinet near the front door, grabbed his deer rifle, and headed out into the early gray dawn.

As he walked across the yard, or what passed for a yard in front of the house, he heard a voice behind him.

"Pa, everything alright?" Freddie asked.

He was Charlie and Lucille's youngest son. He slept in a room near the front door, and it wasn't surprising that he'd heard Charlie go out the door.

"Everything's fine, son," Charlie replied. "I just woke up early and thought I'd walk around and check on things. I think I heard some wolves the other night. I want to make sure they leave the pigs alone."

"Okay, Pa," Fred answered.

"Go get some wood for the stove. Your ma will be up soon and she'll want to make breakfast."

"Yes, sir."

Charlie left the house and walked over to the pigpen, which was more like a mud pit with some dry spots and barbed wire strung around some sticks and logs to keep the pigs in. Most of the pigs were still sleeping.

He glanced over toward the camper trailer where his middle son Billy lived, and then behind it to the mobile home where his oldest son Jesse lived with his wife Sarah and their two kids, Sally and Clinton. An oil lamp was shining in the window of the trailer. *Jesse must be up.*

Charlie turned and started to walk back toward the house. Stopping in the yard, he looked down the long drive as it led to the road beyond. He stood there for a moment, watching.

Clear. No sign of wolves.

With a shrug of his shoulders, he headed toward the house. *Wish we had some coffee…*

As Charlie reached the top step to his front porch, he heard the mechanical sounds of two vehicles coming down the drive toward his house.

He spun around. Black military-looking vehicles.

Charlie's first thought was *What do they call those things—humming, hummers—something like that.*

A man exited the passenger side of the front vehicle, aimed a pistol, and shot Charlie.

Charlie's chest was on fire. Blood was everywhere. He'd been hit twice in the chest. With all his might, he aimed the rifle at the vehicle but couldn't hold on. As he crumpled to the porch, his last thought was of his beautiful Lucille.

*   *   *

"Okay, boys, they're all yours," Jamison shouted. "Do what you want, but no survivors."

"Yes, sir," two men shouted with enthusiasm as they got out of the vehicle and headed for the house.

Jamison saw the small camper beside the house. *I wonder if we could tow that back to the armory. It'd make a nice Commanders Quarters.*

He walked to just a few feet away from the camper when a shot rang out, striking Jamison in the center of his face.

Dropping like a rag doll, Jamison landed in a heap on the ground.

Multiple shots from two FEMA troops from the second HMMWV silenced any more shooting from the camper.

"Go check that camper out!" one man shouted as he knelt next to Jamison, putting his fingers on the man's neck, checking for a pulse. "He's deader'n shit," he remarked as he wiped blood off of his fingers and onto Jamison's shirt.

Two men stopped behind him, staring at their dead leader on the ground.

"Go check out the damn camper," the man ordered, and they scampered away.

Making eye contact with another man who'd run to check on them, he said, "Let's go see what we can find in that trailer. There have to be some women around here."

CHAPTER 6

"Man is the cruelest animal."

—Friedrich Nietzsche

Brian, Rahn, and Jake had established patrol sectors and schedules. I thought it was a sound plan. Jake would assign his people to mounted patrols that utilized logging roads, trails, and through farm pastures. Rahn and Brian would assign patrols for the National Guard soldiers using roads while maintaining one vehicle behind as a quick reaction team, should anyone need help. They would try to get the FEMA HMMWV running and, if not, cannibalize it for parts.

Jake had agreed that his patrols would go out for two to three days at a time. The idea behind it, while they could easily cover more ground, they were also relatively slower. Each of Jakes's teams would be equipped with my BaoFeng UV-82HP high power dual band radios.

The National Guard teams would have their SINCGARS. If communication between the systems became a problem, we had Sam's HAM radio in the barn. He had a significantly longer range and could switch between frequencies and teams. Jake and Brian had made a map, and using numbers to designate the teams, they placed it in Sam's work area so he could more easily understand where everyone was. Sam had become our Operations Hub.

We had gathered by the barn and were distributing ammunition, extra batteries for the BaoFengs, and rations for both the men and horses. It was still summer and the horses could graze. However, making sure they had oats and feed would help keep their strength up. We were sending out four teams with Jake and three with Rahn.

"Okay, everyone, listen up," Brian shouted.

"At ease," Rahn added. Other than the nickering of the horses and rattle of equipment tied to saddles, it was quiet.

"I want everyone to have an idea where each other will be. You have seen the map and you know where your sectors are. Sectors One, Two, and Three are National Guard. They have the roads to Markton, White Lake, and Elton. Jake's teams have sectors Four through Seven. That is the real estate in those areas that is not along the road," Brian instructed. "One team will go west into Sector Four between Elton and Polar. They are our early warning system because the highway from Antigo runs through there."

"Oh, the slacker patrol," one of Jake's men interrupted.

"Knock it off," Jake quickly replied. "Everybody will eventually work every sector; nobody is slacking off."

"If I may," Brian said and continued making eye contact with the outspoken member of Jake's team. "Everyone should easily be within range of the BaoFengs, but just in case, Sam or whoever is in the HAM room will be listening in, and they should pick you up regardless."

Craig, Addie, and Sajan, Craig's best friend from Appleton, were listening through the barn door. Not wanting to be left out, Craig walked over to the group and interrupting Brian, asked, "What about us? We don't want to stay back here and pull guard duty while listening to the HAM radio."

"Don't worry, Craig," Brian answered. "We'll coordinate the guard schedule with patrol schedules. You'll be going out with the National Guard guys."

"When?" Craig asked, his tone challenging.

"More than likely in the next round of patrols," Brian replied. "These guys," he said, pointing at the National Guardsmen, "are trained for this. Youse guys," —I rolled my eyes when he did that; Brian always liked to poke fun at the Wisconsin accent— "have learned on the job. You've done well, Craig, but this situation is getting more difficult. I don't want anyone out there until we know it works. The guard knows what to do."

"Fair enough," Craig said, satisfied for the moment.

"Any other questions?" Brian asked. He scanned the group.

There would be two men for each of the HM-MWVs and two mounted men for each of the horse patrols. The grim looks he had coming his way told him they were ready.

"Okay, last thing," Brian said. "Radio check-ins every hour. Otherwise, radio silence. Once again, your call sign is the Letter S and your sector number. Keep traffic to a minimum. We don't want them finding us because we are chatting. All you need to say is S 1, all clear, or whatever your sector identifier is. Wait for an acknowledgment so that you know it was received. Then shut up. Leave your radios on in case someone has to contact you. Happy hunting, men."

The sounds of the HMMWVs's engines starting up and men mounting horses was all I heard. The vehicles went out first, followed by the horse patrols. Then, all was quiet again.

*　　　*　　　*

"Antigo 6, Antigo 6, this is Antigo Base, over," the young operator said into his handset. "Antigo 6, this is Antigo Base, over? No answer, Edmiston," he explained.

"Try the FEMA Base in Wausau," Edmiston suggested.

"Wausau Base, Wausau Base, this is Antigo Base, over," the operator said.

"Antigo Base, this is Wausau Base, over," the clear voice said through the speaker.

"Wausau, this is Antigo. We are looking for Antigo 6, over."

"Antigo, this is Wausau, hold one."

"I guess they are going to go find him," the operator said to Edmiston.

"How long?" Edmiston asked.

"Depends on where he is, I guess. They probably would have said something if it was going to be awhile," the operator replied.

"We are in deep shit," Edmiston said to no one in particular. They had three men killed in action, one of which was Captain Jamison and one wounded from the raid. They had done what Jamison had told them to do. There were no survivors. The boys had a lot of fun with the woman they'd found in the trailer. Once they threatened to kill her kids, she'd cooperated real good. Then, they killed everyone anyway.

I don't know how Major Wolfe is going to take this. Edmiston looked away from the operator, embarrassed.

"Antigo Base, this is Antigo 6, over," Major Elias Wolfe responded.

Edmiston took the microphone from the operator and said, "Antigo 6, this is Antigo Base. We have a big problem here, over."

"Antigo 6, this is Antigo Base, FEMA 6 is KIA, over."

"Antigo Base, this is Antigo 6, say again last transmission, over."

"Antigo 6, this is Antigo Base, FEMA 6 is KIA, over."

"Shit," Wolfe said loudly. "How the hell did *that* happen?"

"Antigo 6, this is Antigo Base, we were conducting a raid on a farm. He received a gunshot wound, through and through, to the head, over."

"Antigo Base, stand fast, I will be in touch, over."

*   *   *

Sam Karpinski was showing Allen how the HAM worked. Following Allen's injury before the last major battle, it had been decided that until he fully recovered—besides doing guard duty in the bunker—Allen would be a backup for Sam. The HAM radio had been turned on and warmed up for a few minutes and then Sam began to demonstrate how to turn the dials for the various frequencies they used.

"This is the frequency for the FEMA boys over in Antigo," he said. No sooner than those words had left his mouth than Sam heard something coming from thespeaker.

After he made a few very gentle adjustments, the voices came through loud and clear.

"Antigo Base, this is Antigo 6, say again last transmission, over."

"Antigo 6, this is Antigo Base, FEMA 6 is KIA, over."

"Who is Antigo 6 and who is FEMA 6?" Allen asked.

Sam held a finger to his lips.

The radio squawked again with voices. "Antigo 6, this is Antigo Base, we were conducting a raid on a farm. He received a gunshot wound, through and through, to the head, over."

"Holy shit," Sam exclaimed. "Allen, run and get John. Don't say anything to anyone."

Allen hesitated for a minute as if glued in place. "What farm, Sam?"

"Get John now, dammit. NOW!" Sam demanded.

Allen took off, running down the stairs and across the yard until he found John watching Ethan and Caleb playing in the yard with an old soccer ball. Dashing up the steps, Allen shouted, "John, John, Sam needs you in the barn. He needs you now, John."

"What's going on, Allen?"

"He told me not to say. Just to tell you to get to the barn," Allen gasped. He leaned over, hands on his knees and gulped for air.

"You alright?" John asked.

"I'm fine, just outa shape, I guess. A little dizzy from the run, too."

"Stay here and watch these two. Don't let them wander off," John said as he left the porch and headed for the barn.

*   *   *

When I got to Sam's spot in the barn, he told me everything that had been heard over the radio.

"It sounds like that FEMA boy got himself killed," Sam said.

"Right now, I want to know what farm was raided. It would have to be far enough away from here so that we wouldn't hear the shots," I said. I went to the map on the wall Sam used to keep track of the teams and put my finger onto several points on the map.

"There aren't too many people left out here. Just us, the Winstons, and some people down closer to the Rez."

A chill went through me as I said, "I bet it's the Winstons. Tom and Billy Winston had a run-in with some FEMA boys. It has to be the Winstons. Who's in their sector, Sam?"

Sam looked at his list, checked the map, and replied, "Rahn, Johnson, and Schwartz. Hard to break those three up. With Brian's arm in a sling, Rahn said he'd go out periodically."

"Get him on the radio and send him there. I'll get a team together here and if we have to go there, we will," I said as I headed down the stairs.

Behind me, I heard Sam pick up the microphone and say, "S2, S2, this is Base over."

I raced across the yard looking for Brian. By the time I got to the cabin, I noticed he was on the porch. Allen was talking to him. As soon as he saw me, he said, "Get a team together and go."

"I'll take them myself. They don't know where to go. Who's here?"

"Hart and Owens. They worked good together," Brian said. He was standing now and beginning to pace. Brian always paced when he was getting wrapped up into something.

"I'm going to take Donna with me, too," I said.

Craig and several of the National Guardsmen were standing by the HMMWV as I ran up. I knew Owens but couldn't remember Hart, so I called his name.

"Grab your gear. You, too, Owens. We are heading out NOW!" I ordered.

Then, turning to Craig, I said, "Go get your mom. Tell her to grab her kit and get out here now!"

Craig ran toward the house as I started to climb into the HMMWV. Gary came up, having been at the new cabin finishing the construction. "What's going on?" he asked.

"Looks like the Winstons may have been attacked. Sam intercepted a radio message where the FEMA people were talking about a raid. I think it's them," I answered.

"Shit," he replied. "What do you need me to do?"

"Stay here. Be in charge. Other than that, I don't know yet. I'll radio back when we know more."

"You're not going alone, are you?" he asked as Donna came running up.

She had her bag, my AR, and her AR in a sling across her back. She always hated a single point sling, preferring the old style two point.

"You might need this," she said as she handed me my weapon.

All I had was my sidearm, strapped in a leg holster. Hart and Owens had returned and we all climbed into the Hummer.

Hart started it, and we took off.

As we drove past the cabin, I saw Craig, Linda, and Allen standing on the porch, grim looks on their faces.

*   *   *

"S2, S2, this is Base, over," Rahn heard Sam say into the speaker in the humvee.

"Base, this is S2, over," Rahn said.

"S2, Head Honcho is heading your way. Wants to meet at the pig house, over," Sam said.

"Pig house?" Specialist Johnson asked.

"I think he means where we got those pigs," Rahn glanced at him. Keying his SINCGAR, he responded, "Roger, I understand, over."

Setting the radio down, he asked Johnson, "You know where the Winston farm is?"

"Roughly. Heard Craig and the kid, Rick, talk about it once."

"Head over there. John wants to meet us. Schwartz, keep your eyes peeled up there."

"Roger, First Sergeant," Schwartz shouted down from his position in the turret.

Specialist Johnson turned the vehicle around and headed toward the Winston farm. After driving for about 15 minutes, Johnson remarked, "First Sergeant, I think that's John up ahead."

Not too far in the distance was a HMMWV, the SAW plainly visible mounted on top. "Yeah, that's him," Rahn replied.

After a moment, Johnson pulled his vehicle in behind the parked vehicle. Rahn exited through his door and headed toward the passenger side of the other vehicle.

"John, what's going on?" Rahn asked.

*   *   *

Stepping out of the Hummer, I replied, "We think there's been an attack on the Winston's farm. It's about a mile ahead. I wanted us to coordinate and be prepared for what's up there."

"What do you think happened?" Rahn asked.

"Sam intercepted a transmission from the armory to Wolfe in Wausau. It seems they attacked a farm. Jamison was killed."

"Holy shit," Rahn exclaimed. "Jamison took one. Couldn't happen to a nicer guy. Any idea on casualties for the Winstons?"

"No, and that's why we are stopping here. I want everyone locked and loaded when we go in. They'll be trigger happy, and I can't say that I blame them if they are."

"Hey, First Sergeant," Owens said from up in the turret of the Hummer.

"Hello, PFC Owens. Who else you got with you?" Rahn asked as he leaned over to look inside.

"Specialist Hart," I answered. "He and Owens were already experienced together, and I thought it would be wise to keep it that way. Donna is along in case somebody needs a nurse."

"Sounds good. How do you want to do this?"

"I know where I'm going, so I'll lead the way. You follow about 30 feet behind me." I gave RAhn a long look. "Make sure your gunner knows that he needs to be extra alert. The Winstons might shoot first, and we don't need any friendly fire injuries. I'm not expecting any FEMA people, but the Winstons might not see the difference between a black Hummer and one of ours."

"Sounds good. Lead the way," Rahn said.

I nodded at him, and we both got into our vehicles.

*   *   *

Watching John and his group drive away, Craig, Linda, and Allen stood on the porch with worried expressions.

"So what did you hear, Allen?" Craig asked.

"I don't know if I should say," Allen replied.

"C'mon, Allen, we've known each other forever. You can tell me," Craig implored.

Allen hesitated, then said, "Sam overheard a radio call from FEMA. It seems they attacked a farm near here. Their leader was killed, but that's all I know."

"What farm?" Craig asked.

Allen shrugged. "I think it was the Winstons."

"The Winstons?" Linda asked. "The people who gave us the pigs?"

"That would be them," Craig said. "Did they say anything about anyone else being hurt?"

"No, just that it was attacked and their leader was killed," he replied.

"Oh my," Linda said. "This is bad."

"It could be," Craig said. "I'm sure Dad will call in. I'm going by Sam to wait and see." He picked up his AR and left, leaving Allen and Linda alone.

"This is bad, Allen," she said. "This is really bad."

Allen shrugged. "Probably, but we have a lot of support here now. We should be okay."

Linda turned quickly and went into the cabin.

I shouldn't have said anything. The two boys playing with the soccer ball in the yard got Allen's attention. *Guess I'll stand here and watch the kids.*

*   *   *

We turned into the drive leading to the Winstons' home. It was quiet, too quiet actually. "Owens, be on alert," I said loud enough for him to hear over the sound of the engine.

I told Hart to slow down, and we crept forward. The trees on either side of the drive put a dark shadow over the road. The trees cleared, and I saw a body lying on the porch at the front of the Winstons' house. The man was dressed in tan overalls and I recognized him as Charlie.

"This does not look good," Hart said aloud.

"Stop here," I directed. Grabbing my AR, I exited the vehicle and took a minute to scan the area. It was obvious we were alone.

Rahn came up behind us and stopped, too.

"Keep your eyes open, Owens," I said. "Donna, stay in the Hummer until we know what's going on."

I saw her nod her head, then I walked back to speak with Rahn. He had gotten out of his vehicle and we met between the two.

"I think we have a problem here," he said, stating the obvious.

"Yes, we do," I answered. "Hart, check the trailer and camper. Chris, let's go check the house."

"Schwartz, stay alert. Johnson, go with Hart," Rahn said.

The two of us headed toward the house as Hart and Johnson went toward the trailer and camper.

We stopped, and I knelt down next to the body. I rolled it over. "Yep, that's Charlie," I said, confirming my thoughts. He'd been shot through the chest and his body was already cold. "Damn shame. He was a good man."

We silently continued into the house, weapons ready, and lined up with where we were looking. Both of us had our fingers on the trigger.

We cleared the first floor by splitting up. While probably not the safest way to do so, it wasn't a big house. It had a central hallway that went from front to back with two large rooms on either side. I got the dining room and kitchen. Rahn took the living room and what appeared to be a smaller room they used as a laundry room. We met in the hall toward the back of the house.

"Nothing," I said.

"Time to do the hard one; let's go upstairs. We stay together this time," Rahn said.

"I agree," I replied firmly.

We headed toward the stairs, near the front door. They led up to a landing, turned left and then went the rest of the way to the second floor. Rahn led the way as we crept up the stairs.

An occasional squeak of the steps made me jittery. Anyone here would already know we were in the house. Rahn reached the landing, turned, and started up the second set of stairs. He took two steps and said, "I've got another body." Then, stopped.

"Who is it?" I asked and then realized that Rahn had never been here and had only met Charlie, Fred, and Billie when they came to the cabin.

"It's a woman."

"Young or old?"

"Older, gray hair, curled up in a housecoat. She's been shot. I can see it from here."

"That must be Charlie's wife, Lucille. He has a daughter, too."

"Sons as I recall, John."

"Three boys, one's married with two kids. I'm not feeling good about any of this." Those words had no sooner left my mouth, then a long burst of fire from one of our weapons broke the silence.

Rahn and I exchanged a quick glance and ran down the stairs and out the front door.

Owens was still in my vehicle, standing in the turret. He waved us on as we ran across the yard.

I could see Schwartz in the other vehicle looking toward the trailer.

As we got past my vehicle, I saw Donna on the steps of the trailer holding Hart in her arms.

Johnson was standing a few feet away, kicking at the ground.

When we got to Donna and Hart, it was obvious Hart was sobbing. Donna was holding him, rocking back and forth.

"Shhh, shhh," she said softly. She looked up at us and said, "He says it's bad, John."

Rahn and I shared a glance, started up the steps, and stepped around Hart. As Rahn squeezed by him, Hart grabbed his leg. "I'm going to kill them, First Sergeant. I'm going to find them and kill them." Letting go of Rahn's leg, he stood up and walked across the yard.

Donna sat back on the steps and said, "I'm not going back in there, John."

Turning, I pulled the door open and walked into Dante's version of hell.

CHAPTER 7

"...Into the dark, the deep—into evil."

—Friedrich Nietzsche

The small convoy raced up Highway 45 toward Antigo. Major Elias Wolfe, formerly of the Wisconsin Army National Guard and now wearing the black uniform of the FEMA Security Force, rode in the HMMWV leading the army 5-ton truck. Wolfe was with his driver and two other FEMA Security Force members. Mounted in the turret above was an M60 7.62 mm caliber machine gun, a belt of ammunition feeding into it from an ammo box next to it. The truck carried extra ammunition, several cases of M67 hand grenades, and six additional FEMA soldiers.

After reviewing his former National Guard soldiers at the camp in Wausau and discussing them with the FEMA Regional Administrator Rick Barstow, it was decided the soldiers would be better guards at the camps and the FEMA soldiers more appropriate for the task ahead.

Barstow had put Wolfe in charge, provided him with a FEMA commission, and told him to go back to Antigo and "solve the problem." Wolfe was determined to do just that.

A short while later, the convoy rolled into the former armory and stopped in the fenced-off yard. Exiting the vehicle, Wolfe told his driver, "Get this vehicle ready for movement."

"Yes, sir," the driver replied. "When will we be heading out?"

"Soon. I have things to do first."

Wolfe walked back to the 5-ton and told the occupants, "Unload this equipment, get some chow, and be ready." He then went inside the armory and headed toward the communications room.

As he entered, all was quiet. The five operators were sitting around talking with each other, engaging in what Wolfe knew from the army as "smoking and joking."

"You men are going to have to learn to stand up when an officer enters the room," Wolfe said firmly. "I'm in charge now, and this group will be run like an efficient military unit."

The men all stared at him, put out their cigarettes, and stood silently.

"Give me a situation report," Wolfe ordered.

"Sir, there is nothing new to report. We pulled all of the patrols in after your last order. They are in the assembly room, awaiting instructions," one of the operators replied.

Glaring at the man, Wolfe wheeled about and walked out of the room, heading toward the assembly room a short distance away.

Entering it, he saw a repeat of what he had seen in the communications room. The men were all sitting around on cots talking, smoking, and mostly doing nothing.

"Hello, Major," one of the men said, seeing Wolfe come through the door.

"Get these men into some kind of military formation," Wolfe said.

"Sir?" the man replied.

"Get them into a god-damned formation. NOW," Wolfe said sharply.

"Okay, everyone, get into formation," the man hollered.

Most of the men simply looked at him, uncertain of what to do. Eventually, several of the men walked over to an empty area and began to assemble into ranks.

"The major said get in formation," the man shouted.

In a few minutes, all of the FEMA men were standing in a semblance of a military formation with four ranks of five men each.

Wolfe stood in front of them, looked them over, and said, "Men, Rick Barstow, the Regional Administrator, has placed me in charge. From now on, we are going to operate as a military unit. I'll be appointing squad leaders, and you will do as they say. In the next few days, we will take this fight to the people, who through their treason have interfered with our authority, and we will eliminate every one of them. We will make them pay for the death of Captain Jamison."

Wolfe knew that the people who killed Jamison were already dead. He wanted to use the death of their former leader to help inspire and motivate the men. "I will tolerate no disobedience, nor will I tolerate anyone not doing their duty. We are at war with these people, and I intend to win. Where is Edmiston?"

"Right here," Edmiston spoke up.

"Right here, what?" Wolfe barked.

"Um, right here, Major?"

"Good enough. From now on, you will address me as Major or sir. Are there any questions?" Wolfe eyed each of the men.

No one spoke. The men stood silently shuffling their feet. One man, standing in what would be the position of First Squad Leader stood in the at-ease stance. His hands were behind his back, arms loose and feet approximately shoulder-width apart.

"YOU," Wolfe said as he pointed at him. "What's your name?"

"Thomas, sir," he replied.

"That your first or last name?" Wolfe asked.

"Last name, sir," Thomas replied.

"For now, you are the Platoon Sergeant. Get these men working on cleaning weapons, getting their gear squared away, and some of them need showers. They stink," Wolfe said. "You keep the job as long as you measure up. Screw it up, and I'll replace you with someone else."

"Yes, sir," Thomas replied.

"Edmiston, come with me," Wolfe said as he turned and left the assembly room.

*   *   *

The first thing I saw when I entered the trailer was a bloody mass in what was the living room.

"Jesus," Rahn said as he entered behind me. The body was obviously male and had literally been shot to pieces.

"That must be Jesse," I said aloud. "He had a wife and two kids." Hesitantly, I walked toward the back of the trailer. There were two bedrooms on one side of the hall and a bathroom. All empty.

We entered the back bedroom, and the bile instantly rose up in my throat. I retched and took a step backward, bumping into Rahn. Taking a moment to take a few quick breaths, I re-entered the bedroom. The naked body of a woman was tied to the bed. It was obvious she'd been raped. She had what appeared to be several bullet wounds in her chest and had been shot in the face as well.

"Mother fucker," Rahn mumbled behind me.

We stood there, too stunned to move.

"I haven't seen anything like this since Iraq," Rahn said, the emotion clear in his voice as he choked on his words.

I turned my eyes away from her, and as I did so, I noticed a small foot on the far side of the bed. Slowly approaching it, the horror continued. Lying on the floor were two children, their throats cut.

I could only imagine the horrors that had gone on in this room. How afraid they were. I grabbed a blanket off of the floor and tossed it over the bodies. Then, the bile rose again and I began to retch.

Turning, I raced out of the room, down the hall, and out of the trailer. I didn't get far before I puked my guts out.

Rahn came up behind me, placing his hand on my shoulder. He said nothing.

I continued with a few dry heaves before my stomach settled down, my hands on my thighs and my body bent over. Bits of vomit was on my boots and pants. I felt a tap and saw that Rahn was handing me his canteen.

I took it, nodding my head in thanks. I took a swig and swished it around, spitting the water onto the ground. I took another drink, this time swallowing. I gave it back to him, and said, "There are two more boys and a girl. Charlie had three sons and a daughter."

"Johnson, take Hart back to the Hummer and send Schwartz over here."

"Yes, First Sergeant," he replied.

A moment later, PFC Schwartz came up to Rahn. "Yes, First Sergeant."

"We have two men and a girl that are unaccounted for. We're going to check the camper."

Schwartz noticeably swallowed and said, "Yes, First Sergeant."

The two men headed toward the camper, and I saw them enter it. They came back out a moment later. Rahn held up one finger, letting me know there was a body in there.

When he got close enough to me to not have to shout, he said softly, "One male body, must be the other son."

Hope filled me. "That means the girl and another son is missing. We have to find them."

"Johnson, Schwartz! Front and center!" Rahn shouted.

The two soldiers swiftly approached Rahn and stopped a few feet away. "Yes, First Sergeant," they said almost simultaneously.

"Go search the house from basement to attic, every room and under every piece of furniture. You're looking for a girl and another man." He stopped, looked toward me and asked, "How old?"

"I'm guessing she's about fourteen, five feet and a little bit, with brown hair," I answered.

"She's probably scared to death, so be careful. If the son is out there, he might be a bigger issue. The Winstons knew how to use guns," Rahn finished.

"Yes, First Sergeant," the two men replied and headed off toward the house, giving Charlie's body a wide berth when they reached the porch.

"Owens, you stay on that weapon. Anyone comes up on us that you don't know, stop them," I shouted.

"Yes, sir, Mr. Henry," Owens replied.

*   *   *

Edmiston and Wolfe entered the office that was once again Wolfe's. Edmiston closed the door.

"Tell me what happened," Wolfe said.

"Captain Jamison gathered us up—there were seven of us—and we went to the farm that belonged to those people we took the turkeys from."

"I remember," Wolfe interrupted. "Continue."

"The captain said we were to take no prisoners and that we could have some fun, do what we wanted. We got to the farm, and one of them, an old man, was walking up the steps of the house. When we pulled up, the old guy stopped and faced us. The captain got out and shot him twice. Then, he told us to go have fun.

"The captain walked toward a camper. He didn't get far before somebody started shooting from a window in the camper, and the captain was killed. We shot up the camper pretty bad and then went to the trailer while the other guys were heading toward the house. There was a shot from outside the house, but it missed. We found that guy and Minster killed him."

"Minster?" Wolfe said.

"Yeah, sick fucker. We were shot at from the trailer, but we took him out easy. The dumb shit stood in an open door. He wounded Bodine, just a graze in the side, got under his vest. We went into the trailer and found a woman with two kids. Bodine was pissed and was gonna shoot the kids, but I said no. We told the woman that if she did as we said we wouldn't hurt the kids. She agreed. We tied her up and took turns. There was some gunfire, and because I was done, I went and checked.

"Minster had killed an old woman, probably the old guy's wife, and he and Clifton were coming out the front door. I told 'em what we had in the trailer, and that's where they went. Minster was last, and he was pissed about that. So, he took the kids and slit their throats in front of the woman. Then, he shot her."

"You all raped that woman?" Wolfe said.

"Yes, sir. Captain Jamison said we could."

"Let me be real clear, Edmiston. If I find out you or anybody else rapes another woman, I will personally execute you on the spot, do you understand?"

"Sir, Captain Jamison said…"

"I don't give a shit what the captain said; he's dead. I'm in charge now. There will be no rape. Do I make myself clear?"

"Yes, sir."

"Now, get the hell out of my office!"

"Yes, sir." Edmiston walked quickly out of the office, closing the door behind him.

Wolfe stared at the closed door. *What the hell am I doing, and what have I gotten myself into? I should have Minster executed to make a point. If I do that, though, they'll think I'm weak. Fuck it. We're at war with these people, and I'm gonna be at the top when this is all over.*"

*   *   *

"How's Hart?" Rahn asked.

"Donna's with him. You heard what he said when we went in the trailer. Can't say I disagree with him, either," I answered.

"Why don't you stay here? I'll go help them look for the other two," Rahn offered.

"Okay," I said, and went over to help Donna with Hart. I didn't get very far because she held her hand up in a stop motion.

I stood there for a second and decided to look around the rest of the yard and buildings. I didn't think any of the FEMA people were here anymore, but if either of the two Winstons we were looking for had a weapon, I was pretty sure I'd be shot at. So I walked slow and kept my head on a swivel.

I went over to where the pigs were. They had all been shot and were lying in the mud.

Leaving the pigpen, I went around the side of the house and found the remaining son. He'd been shot, once full in the face.

I heard Rahn shout my name and went to the front of the house.

Standing in the front doorway, he said, "We found her. Get Donna."

"She alright?" I asked and then realized that was a dumb ass question. I called for Donna, and she pulled herself away from Hart and came running over.

"They found the girl. They need you."

Donna ran to the house.

Rahn stopped her at the door and said, "She's upstairs. She's a mess. They didn't do anything to her, though."

With a grim look on her face, Donna went upstairs. They'd found her hiding in a small closet that ran along the wall. She was still there when Donna arrived.

"She's in the closet," Schwartz said. "Her name's Emma. She's hysterical. Figured a woman could help better."

"You did good, Jay," Donna replied. She dropped to her hands and knees and crawled into the closet, where she found Emma curled up in the back, rocking back and forth.

"Hi, Emma. My name is Donna."

Emma continued to rock, but her eyes locked onto Donna as she continued to crawl closer.

Not wanting to get too close and scare her, Donna stopped and put herself in a sitting position. She sat silently for a few minutes, waiting to see the girl's reaction.

After a while, Emma said, "They shot my mom."

"Yes, honey, they did. I am so sorry," Donna answered softly. It was all she could do to keep the emotion out of her voice and remain calm.

"Why did they shoot my mom?"

"I don't know. Bad people do bad things some-times, and we can't stop them."

"Mom saved me. She made me go in here. I heard them shoot her...and they laughed," she said.

Crying now, Emma screamed, "They shot my mom and they laughed." She began to sob heavily.

Donna slid across the floor and got next to the girl, putting her arm around her and holding her.

"Why did they shoot my mom?" she cried.

Donna continued to hold her, stroking her hair and rocking with her.

I came upstairs and saw Owens and Schwartz sitting on the bed, unsure of what to do.

"Where is she?" I asked softly.

"In there," Schwartz answered, pointing toward the small door that led into the closet.

"Why don't you two take the sheet off this bed, cover up Mrs. Winston and take her outside where Emma won't see her."

"Yes sir," they both said, and stood up and did as they had been told.

I sat on the bed and waited.

CHAPTER 8

*"To make it right, pain and suffering is the key
to all windows,
without it, there is no way of life."*

—Helen Keller

I sent Donna back with Emma, Schwartz, Hart, and Johnson. Rahn, Owens, and I remained behind. We had the tough task of taking care of the bodies. After some discussion, we decided to put them all together in the backroom of the trailer and burn it down. We couldn't bury them, as all we had were the pioneer tools from the HMMWV and Charlie didn't have any shovels on the farm. If we didn't bury them, the scavengers would get them.

Tying bandanas around our faces, we carried Billy, Fred, and Lucille into the trailer. And lastly, we brought in Charlie and laid him next to Lucille. Rahn picked up the children and gently lay them next to their mother, who had been untied and covered.

Owens had found a 5 gallon can of gasoline, and we poured it over them before leaving the trailer.

Rahn wrapped a rag around a stick, soaked it in the gas, and then went back inside, lighting it and tossing it down the hall. With a loud whoosh, it ignited. And he ran outside.

We stayed for a while and let it burn. Just as we were getting ready to leave, two of the guys from the Rez rode up.

"Hey, Mr. Henry, we saw the smoke," one of them said.

I didn't feel like correcting them about my name. I didn't feel like a lot of things right now. I took a few minutes to explain to them what happened.

"Shit just got more real, Mr. Henry."

"Yes, it did," I answered. "I'm sorry I didn't get your name."

"I'm Ray, and this is Charlie," he answered, pointing at his partner.

"Did you guys hear any shooting yesterday?"

"No, we were several miles from here and were just scouting this area when we saw the smoke.

Saw your vehicle and figured it was somebody on our side," Ray said.

"Well, be careful identifying friend or foe by these vehicles," I said. "The other side has them, too, and it could be a fatal mistake."

"Good point," Ray said.

"When are you two heading back in?" I asked.

"Just as soon as we meet up with our relief. That will be tomorrow."

I nodded. "Stay safe then. See you back at the cabin."

"Hope so," he replied. They turned their horses and trotted off.

I went to the HMMWV. Rahn was already in the driver's seat.

"You obviously are driving," I said.

"You have a military driver's license?" he questioned.

"I'm sure in a box back in the cabin."

"It's probably expired then."

I smiled for the first time all day as I walked around and climbed in the front passenger seat. It wasn't a big smile, but the small one that it was gave me hope. "Let's go home," I said.

*   *   *

Donna took Emma to the room that she shared with Craig, telling him that he'd have to sleep in the barn for a while. The confused look on his face made her stop and she said, "I'll explain later. Just go find Sajan or Allen and tell them you'll be bunking with them for a bit."

"Okay," was all he said.

Linda came into the cabin and went upstairs. Walking down the hall, she stopped in front of Donna's bedroom door and tapped lightly. Placing her ear close to the door, she heard a slight shuffling of feet, and then the door opened a small crack.

A whispered voice asked, "Who is it?"

"Hi Donna, it's me, Linda, can I come in?"

Donna opened the door and motioned for Linda to come in. She put her finger to her lips, indicating she didn't need Linda to talk at the moment and then closed the door behind her.

A blanket covered the girl who was on Donna's bed, a patchwork quilt over the top of her, even now in the middle of summer. Emma lay in the bed, quiet, not moving, and with her back toward the two women.

Again putting her finger to her lips, Donna went over to Emma, leaned over and said softly, "We are going to step out in the hall. I'll leave the door open slightly, and if you need me, just call."

The response from Emma was a slight shifting of her body on the bed as she pulled the quilt up around her neck and appeared to hug a bolster pillow that was under the quilt with her.

Donna motioned for Linda to follow her, and the two women stepped out into the hall.

Whispering, Linda said, "Everyone is talking crazy outside. Hart is telling horrible stories, the guys are getting mad, and Brian is about to lose control of them. What's going on?"

Donna took a few minutes to describe what had happened at the Winston's as Linda, her eyes widening in horror as they filled with tears, listened.

"Oh my God," Linda said as she raised her open hand toward her mouth. "Was she…" Linda started to ask.

"No, she hid in a closet and they didn't know she was there. That saved her life. Thank God they didn't decide to search everything," Donna said, interrupting.

"Oh," Linda replied in a small voice. The look in her eyes projected both her relief and concern. "How can I help?"

"Let's go inside so that I can introduce you to her. I think she needs that. Then, I have to go outside and jerk a knot in those boys to calm them down unless John and Rahn get back first."

*   *   *

The heavy stomping of boots on the tiled floor announced someone very angry was coming down the hall. Wolfe had almost torn the door to his office off of its hinges as he opened it when he decided on his next course of action. *I have to send a message that I am in charge and ruthless.*

Entering the assembly room, he saw a group of men in a corner appearing to be cleaning weapons. The rest were still lounging around on their cots.

"PLATOON SERGEANT THOMAS!" Wolfe shouted loudly, seeing what he believed to be a clear violation of his instructions.

A man stood up from the group cleaning weapons and ran over toward Wolfe. "Yes sir," he said, stopping and coming to the military position of attention.

"Get these men into formation now. And those men," he said, pointing at the few lounging on their cots. "Why are they there?"

"They refused to follow my directives, sir," Platoon Sergeant Thomas said.

"Get the men in formation, Sergeant."

"Yes, sir. All right, men, fall in," Thomas ordered.

The group in the back, quick to respond, jogged to the center of the room and began to assemble as instructed.

The five men on their cots were not as enthusiastic in their approach. They walked slowly toward the group, and just as they were close, Wolfe shouted, "You five, stop right there."

The men glanced at each other in confusion.

"Stand next to Sergeant Thomas," Wolfe directed.

Again, the men slowly obeyed.

Wolfe went to the front of the formation when Sergeant Thomas turned to face him, saluted, and said, "Sir, the command is formed."

Returning the salute, Wolfe told the men to stand at ease. Facing the five men next to Sergeant Thomas, he asked, "Tell me your names."

In turn, they responded. Jackson, Meeks, Minster. At the name Minster, Wolfe shouted, "Stop!"

He quickly went and stood in front of Minster. "Did you say Minster?" Wolfe said in an angry but low voice.

"Yup, that's my name," the man answered.

With almost lightning speed, Wolfe pulled his M9 from his leg holster and jammed the barrel under Minster's chin, pushing his head back and causing the man to stagger slightly to keep his balance.

"Jesus Christ," Minster said as loud as he could with the weapon pushing his mouth closed.

"No, I'm Major Wolfe. I just became your worst nightmare," Wolfe said through gritted teeth.

Keeping the pistol hard against Minster's chin, Wolfe said to the group, "This piece of shit thinks he can write his own rules. He thinks he can do what he wants. He thinks he's better than the rest of you. He isn't. He's a piece of shit that is forever on my shit list." He let the words sink in as he slowly moved his gaze across the group of men frozen in place.

"He makes a mistake that gets someone hurt and I will shoot him dead on the spot. He disobeys an order, and I will shoot him dead on the spot. Am I clear?" He paused and waited. "I said, am I clear?" This time Wolfe shouted.

The responses trickled back. "Yes, sir." "Yes, Major."

"Are you people not hearing me? I said, am I clear?" Wolfe shouted, his loud voice echoing off of the walls of the assembly room.

"YES, SIR!" the men shouted back.

"Good," Wolfe said aloud.

Moving his face to within inches of Minster's, he said in a low voice, "Am I clear, you piece of shit?"

"Yes, sir," Minster's trembling reply forced itself out of his mouth.

Wolfe lowered the weapon but kept it in his hand. He backed up a few steps and turned to face the rest of his team. "I will not tolerate disobedience. I will not tolerate less than quick compliance with my orders or the orders of those I have chosen to lead you. Disobey, and punishment will be swift. Sergeant Thomas."

"Yes, sir."

"Take two men, take this piece of shit outside," he said, pointing at Minster. "Strip him and lock him inside one of the empty Conexes in the yard. Give him a canteen of water and nothing more."

"Yes, sir. And the others, sir?" Thomas asked, pointing at the other four men.

"I leave that to your imagination, Sergeant. Impress me with what you've learned over the years. Don't let me see you be weak."

*   *   *

We pulled into the drive to the cabin. No one had said a word the entire way back. Owens was in the turret, and as far as I knew, he was alone with his thoughts up there. Rahn and I stared at the road ahead of us. I guess we were alone with our thoughts, too.

That all changed when the barn came into view and I saw a group of angry men shouting at Craig and Brian. Or rather, Brian was shouting back at them. He did not look pleased.

While his arm was no longer in a sling, the splinted and wrapped arm was flailing wildly as he was saying something to the group.

"What the hell..." Rahn said. The first words he'd spoken since we left the Winston's. He slammed the brakes and turned off the vehicle, jumping out all in one motion. He ran to the group and shouted, "What in the fuck are you people doing? This is your commander, show some god-damned respect."

The silence was immediate.

As I got out of the Hummer and started toward the group, Donna came out of the front door and headed toward us. She looked like a woman on a mission. She was marching with determination. I knew that look.

I veered toward her to intercept her, and she said, "Don't start, John, they need to hear this."

Being the wise man that I am and wanting to live a long life, I stepped aside.

Before she even reached them, she was yelling. "What is wrong with you people? There is a young girl upstairs traumatized over what happened today and you are out here acting like a gang of thugs. She can hear you, and you aren't helping."

If silence can get any deeper, it was at that moment. She got right up into the group and glared at each of them. It was THAT glare. The one that every son and husband knows all too well. Mom was mad, and we were not going to come out on top in this one.

I barely heard her words because I tuned her out. Not because I thought she was wrong, but because I didn't want to suffer the fear that would come from those words.

Then, it got worse. Nancy showed up, and no one can get mad like Nancy. When the two of them started finishing each other's sentences and Nancy started using the stick she sometimes used to help her walk by swinging it like a lecturer's pointer, I stepped back.

"I got this, ladies," Brian said. It didn't help that he smirked.

They turned on him, much to the relief of everyone there. Donna and Nancy proceeded to chew out Brian, raking him with words as he cowered as only Brian can, with great exaggeration.

I think he realized how bad he'd screwed up when Nancy whacked him with her stick. It wasn't a little whack, either, because she hit him in the leg. I swear he almost went down.

"That hurt dammit," he yelled.

That seemed to diffuse everything. Rahn looked as if he was about to laugh out loud.

Owens was smart enough to have never left the Hummer. The other men started to slowly walk away backward, distancing themselves from Nancy the madwoman and her stick. Soon, it was Brian, a very quiet Craig, me, Donna, and Nancy alone on the porch.

My courage returning, I approached them but stood by silently.

"What were you thinking, Brian?" Nancy asked, her anger leaving as fast as it surfaced.

Brian glared at her. "I'm as mad as they are. I stopped them from getting in a vehicle and heading to Antigo. They were going to attack the armory."

Then, First Sergeant Rahn showed up. He yelled, "They are men, Nancy. Sometimes that's how we express ourselves. We shout, yell, and get mad. Then, we calm down."

That quieted them down.

"Yeah, and sometimes you shout, yell, and go off to do something stupid," she replied. "I'm not burying a husband because he got mad and went and did something stupid."

"Actually, that's not a bad idea," I interjected.

All of them turned and looked at me.

"I knew you could be crazy sometimes, John," Donna said. "But sometimes, you can be plain stupid. We can't attack the armory. You said yourself that we don't have enough people or firepower."

"We have enough for a quick raid. A team can sneak into town, raise hell with them, take out some of their weapons, and let them know they aren't safe, either."

"What do you mean, Dad?" Brian asked.

"Just what I said. A small team raids the armory, shoots the shit out of it, uses some of those grenades we have, and sends Wolfe and his men a message."

"That doesn't sound like a bad idea," Rahn said. "We'll need to scout it out, get a good sketch of how they've set it up."

"You people have lost your minds." Donna threw her hands up in the air in exasperation. "What if you get caught?"

"We won't get caught, Mom," Craig replied. "Brian can't go, his arm is still broke. Rahn's men can go. I can go."

"Oh, for Christ's sake," Donna said, anger and frustration showing in her voice. "I'm not going to stand here and listen to this foolishness." She stomped off toward the house.

"It's not a *bad* idea, John," Rahn said.

Nancy frowned at him and turning, followed Donna into the cabin.

Continuing on, Rahn said, "I can lead a small team to scout it out, come back, and we can plan the operation. Two or three of us should be enough for the scout."

"What's the risk factor?" Brian asked. He had returned to being the commander.

"With a small group, one that hides on the edge of town and then hoofs it to the armory can set up for a day and observe what they are doing. Then, we sneak out and return here. It shouldn't be too high."

"Who's on the team?" Brian asked.

He shrugged. "Me, Johnson, maybe Rambo and one other."

"Rambo?" I asked.

"Roop," Brian and Rahn both said.

"He's tougher than he looks," Rahn added.

"I'll go," Craig replied.

"The hell you will," I said. "You aren't trained for it."

"I can do it, Dad. Let me be a part of this. I don't just want to sit in the bunker and watch a few people walk by every other day."

"He can do it, Dad," Brian interjected. "He listens good and he doesn't do stupid shit."

"This isn't hiding in an attic and sniping at people," I said. "This could get real bad if things go south."

"I'll be there, John," Rahn said. "I trust him. I'll keep an eye on him."

"You all seem to be of the same mind. I can't argue with all of you," I said, surrendering quicker than I'd liked. "Have at it then. Just don't fuck it up."

I left them to their planning. It was obvious that I wasn't as much in charge as I thought. Youth and new skills had replaced me.

Maybe that was a good thing; I don't know. I didn't like it, but I realized I couldn't change it.

CHAPTER 9

"In this world, there are tigers. Sometimes, fathers must send their sons with tiger guns to slay those tigers."

—John Henry

It had ended up as a quiet day at the cabin. Everyone knew a mission was being planned— the who and what wasn't to be announced until evening. Even with the quiet, the tension was everywhere. It seemed Donna, Nancy, Linda, and Addie were either mad or worried. Most likely both, plus some other emotions I didn't want to consider. Those not working were lounging around. Some in the barn and others here, with me, on the porch as it was close enough time-wise to call it our regular evening meeting.

Besides the ladies and three kids, Rahn, Brian, Craig, Johnson, Gary, Jake, and me were somewhere situated on the porch. Sajan and Rick were on guard. Sam was at his Ham, and Allen was with his new buddies, the National Guard guys.

Brian announced that Rahn, Craig, Johnson, and Roop had a mission during our evening gathering. They would leave at midnight.

"We're going to get as close as we can to the armory and observe for a day, then return," Rahn explained.

"It sounds dangerous," Addie said. The nervousness in her voice told me everything that many of the others were also feeling.

"We'll be okay, Addie," Craig said. He was sitting next to her and put his arm around her.

She pulled herself closer to him and buried her face in his chest.

"It'll be the four of them," Brian explained. "We need to know their routines, what they're doing, and how they have set themselves up around the armory."

"That sounds like a bit more than just observing," Donna remarked. "I was in the army, too. It sounds like a scouting mission for an operation. What's going on?" She looked toward me.

Brian answered for me. "Our plan is to raid them with a bit of shock and awe. We need to know the set up first."

"You're going to raid them, with four people?" Linda asked.

"No, they're going to scout the armory out, map as much as they can, and then come back here. The raid will happen later," Brian explained. "We aren't going in there blind because we don't know what they have."

"Why?" Linda asked.

"After what happened at the Winston's, it's obvious they feel they have more control than we want them to have. If we can do some serious damage, destroy some vehicles, maybe even kill some of them, we'll make them respect us more."

"Won't that make them come after us even harder, though?" Linda continued her questioning.

Brian lifted his good shoulder in a half shrug. "Maybe, and if they do, we'll be ready for them. Angry people do stupid things. When they act on emotion, they don't think. That will be our advantage."

"So they'll attack us here. What about the kids? We have three little kids here, what about them?" Linda said, her voice rising.

"We'll have a welcoming committee far away from Home Base. There are only a couple of ways they can get here, and we can cover those paths. If we do it right, we can even drive them toward one way and set them up."

"How do you do that?" she asked.

"Just like we used the claymores the last time we were attacked. Linda, you weren't here then, but we used claymore mines to drive the attacking force into a space where we wanted them. We created a kill zone and wiped them out."

"These people could be better trained," Nancy interjected as she rubbed her head. "We won't just have people wounded this time. You know that, Brian."

"And *we* are better trained," Brian insisted, "with soldiers who know what they are doing."

I jumped in. I had a hard time not talking in conversations and wasn't always a good observer. "The National Guard soldiers have been trained in ambushes and combat operations. They are all infantrymen, and they know what to do."

Before I could continue to comfort Linda, two horses cantered into view on the drive. It was Ray and Charlie, returning from their scout.

I waved at them to come over to the porch.

Turning their horses, they approached us, stopping, then dismounting.

Jake stood up at the same time I did, and we went toward them.

"Hi, Jake, Mr. Henry," Ray said.

"It's John," I commented without thinking.

"You folks having a pow-wow?" he asked with a grin.

"We were talking about a team we're sending out to scout the armory in Antigo," Jake said.

"That sounds fun, who's going?" Ray asked.

"We have four people, just enough," I said.

"And you aren't one of them, Ray, so don't even think about asking," Jake added, giving him a stern look.

"I'm not, I'm looking forward to sleeping without bugs buzzing in my ears," he quickly said. "I've got skeeter bites in places that just aren't right."

"C'mon up on the porch and meet everyone," I said.

Ray gave the reins of his horse to Charlie and followed us to the porch.

"Everyone, this is Ray," I said as we went up the steps. I then took a minute to go around the group gathered and introduced everyone there.

"That's a lot of names to remember. I've met some of you, but it's nice to meet all of you," he said.

"Oh, this isn't everyone. We have Sam up in the barn listening to his Ham radio, Sajan is in the bunker out front and Rick's out back. Plus, we have three teams out in Hummers and several soldiers hanging out by the barn or finishing up the cabins," I replied.

"I've met most of the soldiers. Good guys, lots of fun to sit around and bull sh… Sorry, ladies," Ray said as he acknowledged them and the three kids sitting there.

Mike started to giggle. "I know what he was going to say. Dad and Uncle Craig say that alllll the time."

"Yes, and you aren't going to say that word, are you?" Nancy firmly asked.

"No, Ma'am," Mike said, but he was still smiling. His vocabulary had increased significantly with the addition of the soldiers, and of course, Uncle Craig.

"I guess I should be going. I gotta put these horses up and get something for Charlie and me to eat. Nice meeting you folks," Ray said as he tipped his green and gold football hat and walked toward the barn.

*   *   *

The door to the Conex opened with a creak. Minster was lying on the floor in a half-fetal position. His naked body glistened with sweat. Platoon Sergeant Thomas walked in with a galvanized bucket filled with water and threw the water onto Minster, causing him to curl up and shout, "Fuck!"

"Get up, shit bird, you're back inside now," Thomas ordered. His voice was somewhere between disgust and anger.

Kicking Minster's feet with his boot, Thomas again said, "Get up!"

Minster stirred and rolled over, using his arms to push himself up slowly. "Where are my clothes?" he demanded.

"Out here. Get dressed and come into the assembly hall. You two," he said, pointing at the two FEMA men with him, "make sure he gets dressed and comes inside."

They both nodded their heads in acknowledgment.

Thomas turned and went back inside the armory.

*   *   *

"You better do as the sergeant says, Corey," one of the men remarked. "They aren't playing games. I heard the major say a couple of times that he should have shot you."

"Fuck him and fuck Thomas, too," Minster replied as he staggered outside into the evening shade and got dressed. "These guys are cray-cray. All I did was what Jamison said, and then that damn major with the corn cob up his ass gets all high and mighty."

"It ain't like it used to be. If you want to live, maybe you should just play the game," the other FEMA man said.

"Yeah, I'll play their game, for now," Minster replied. Finishing tying his boots, he followed the two men inside. "I'm hungry. Is there chow?"

"Yeah, you get an MRE, just like the rest of us," one of the men said.

"Wonderful. Fucking wonderful," Minster remarked as they entered the building.

The chatter in the assembly room calmed noticeably when the three men entered. Almost everyone stared at them as Minster headed for his cot and sat down, grabbing the tan MRE bag and opening it.

"Wonderful," he said. "Vegetable crumbles with pasta. Anybody wanna trade? I need some meat."

When no one answered, he mumbled, "Assholes." Without even bothering to open the entrée, he proceeded to eat the chunky peanut butter and crackers that came with the meal.

This doesn't even have a good drink mix in it. I'm not drinking this damn cappuccino crap.

Settling for his canteen and the lukewarm water inside it, he continued to eat, all the while muttering to himself.

After he finished eating, he tossed the bag and the contents he didn't eat on the floor.

"I wouldn't do that," the man on the cot next to him said. "Sergeant Thomas will be on your ass in no time, and then it will be hard on the rest of us for letting you do that."

"Fuck this shit," Minster said. Standing up, he picked up the bag and walked over to the garbage can and tossed the bag inside.

When he got back to his cot, he said, "When did you guys get so obedient and shit? This is starting to look like the army. I had enough of that when I was in."

"When were *you* in the army, Minster?" the man asked, the sarcasm in his voice almost palatable.

"Couple of years ago. It was a joke, so I got out."

"Got out or got *kicked* out?" the man said with a smirk.

"Same thing, doesn't matter," Minster answered. "So, what do they have us doing now?"

"Training on what the sergeant calls squad tactics."

"I guess I am back in the army. I need to get out of here. This is bullshit," Minster said as he laid down on his cot. He put his hands behind his head, closed his eyes, and tried to sleep.

His last conscious thought was, *I gotta get out of this chicken outfit.*

*   *   *

After our gathering broke up on the porch, most everyone went to bed. Donna and Linda went to check on Emma, and then, it was just the dogs and me. Rahn went to check on equipment he needed for later tonight and Johnson went with him.

I watched Addie and Craig wander off toward the cabins. I knew Craig had been sneaking over there and spending the night. I figured it might happen when I put him, Sajan, and Allen in the other half of the cabin where she stayed. I certainly hoped they were taking precautions. I know I didn't have anything they could use, and I doubted if any one else did. None of my business—unless we all got a big surprise. That was something we didn't need.

It was too early for a cigar, and Brian had been watching me closely. I knew he wanted to know where I had them stashed. I decided I'd stick my legs out, close my eyes, and look at the moon. No one was letting me do anything anyway.

*   *   *

"I'm worried, Craig," Addie said as they sat in the breezeway of her cabin.

"It will be okay. Rahn knows what he's doing, and I've learned a lot. We won't do anything stupid."

"But why do *you* have to go?"

"We can't let the National Guard guys do everything. Dad, Brian, and Rahn talked it over. Some of us were saying we needed to be more involved. It's what we have to do, Addie. This is for us, too."

"I get it, but I don't have to like it."

"I'll be fine. Don't worry." He squeezed her shoulder.

"Let's go inside," she said as she stood and lightly traced her fingers through his thick, long hair.

"You don't have to ask me twice," he replied with a smirk.

"Jerk," she said with a giggle, but pulled him inside the cabin.

*   *   *

The team left just before midnight. It took them little time to reach the outskirts of Antigo. They drove to the Langlade County Airport and then went cross country, heading north to avoid a small cluster of homes. Then, across unplowed farm fields, eventually hiding the Hummer in a small patch of woods behind a container company near a closed Fleet Farm store.

"Alright, this is what we'll do," Rahn said. "Johnson, I know you won't like this, but you stay here with the Hummer for security. Keep your radio on and stay quiet."

"Yes, First Sergeant," he answered, the unhappiness with the decision clear in his voice.

"If we need you, then you haul ass and find us. You're the best driver, and you know this vehicle and the community," Rahn continued.

"I get it. I don't like it, but I get it," Johnson said.

"We'll cut through these woods, parallel Rusch Road by using the businesses north of it as cover until we cross Highway 47 by the hair studio. There's a patch of woods behind it. We can use those woods to get to another group of woods behind the Best Value Motel, and those woods are behind the back of the armory. We'll position ourselves there in those woods. We'll watch them during the day, keeping track of guard posts, how often they change guards, and try to get an idea of how many people they have. Roop, you'll be rear security. Craig, you'll observe with me. I want to show you how to use the An-PVS14 NVG. It's pretty simple, and it's a passive device."

"What's a passive device?" Craig asked.

"Basically, it means that it's infrared signature only shows up when you are actively using it. Now, let's go. We don't have much time, and we need to be set up in the woods before sunrise."

"Sounds good," Craig replied.

Roop acknowledged the words with a nod of his head and a whispered "Hooah."

"Stay alert, Johnson," Rahn remarked as he led the way through the cluster of trees and bushes toward Rusch Road and their first challenge, staying concealed and crossing Highway 47.

The process was slow as Rahn used the take-a-few-steps, stop-and-listen approach. It took almost an hour for them to reach the side of what had been a jewelry store. The windows were all broken out, the door off of its hinges, and trash strewn everywhere.

Kneeling alongside, Rahn took out his NVG and, using it like a telescope, surveyed the area across the street, their next destination being a small cluster of trees just behind a hair studio about 200 yards away. "We'll have to run across the road. You up for that, Craig," he remarked, the white of his teeth showing in his grin and the camouflaged paint they all had on their faces.

"I got it, Rahn," Craig whispered back. "I'm not as old as you."

"Okay, you go first, then Roop and I'll follow. When you get into those trees, get down behind one of them and keep your head on a swivel."

"Just let me know when," Craig said.

Rahn took out the NVGs and made another sweep of the area. Seeing nothing, he lightly slapped Craig on his shoulder and quietly said, "Go!"

Craig took off, running as fast as he could. It wasn't long before he was across the road and in the trees.

Rahn waited a few minutes and again put the NVG to his eyes and scanned the area. "You ready, Rambo?" he asked.

It had become Roop's nickname after the first contact with the FEMA troops in Lake View at the Quik Mart.

"Roger that," Roop answered.

"Don't trip over Craig. When you get there, get down, and you two divide up where you will watch. I'll be over directly," Rahn added.

Tapping his hand on Roop's shoulder, he whispered, "Go!"

Roop took off across the road, joining Craig.

Rahn waited a few minutes to make sure they hadn't been seen by anyone he had missed. He took one more quick look with the NVGs, and then ran across the road.

Joining up with Roop and Craig, he motioned for them to all get closer. Lying on the ground, Rahn explained, "Okay, we're gonna go through these woods, slow and listening. We'll stop just before we break into the field. Check things out, and then go south toward the woods behind the armory. We'll go low and slow for that. I don't think they're smart enough to put a listening post or an outpost in those woods, but I don't want to make the mistake of underestimating them."

Craig and Roop both nodded their heads.

"I'll lead, and you two—Craig and then Roop—follow me about ten feet apart. You stop when I stop, you get down when I get down. Any questions?"

Neither Craig nor Roop had any.

"Okay, let's go," Rahn said as he stood up, put his weapon at a low ready position, and started toward the woods.

After a few minutes, Craig followed and then Roop. About 30 minutes later, they arrived at the edge. Everyone kneeled and waited while Rahn checked the area.

Raising his arm, he motioned for them to follow him. Repeating their order, they followed him as he turned south, went about 300 yards, and entered the woods behind the armory.

Just inside the tree line, Rahn stopped and motioned everyone to gather around him. "Okay, Roop, you stay here and keep an eye out for anything. No shooting unless you have to. I doubt anyone will be back here, but unless they look like they are going to come in the woods, just observe. Craig and I will move forward. It's about one hundred yards to the other edge."

"Roger, First Sergeant," Roop answered.

"Craig, we'll stop about ten yards from the other edge and low crawl forward. Stay behind me all the way."

"Roger, First Sergeant," Craig replied.

"If only I could get your brother to do that," Rahn said with a smile. "Let's go."

*   *   *

It was quiet inside the assembly room. The only sounds were snores and the occasional fart. Minster had awakened and getting up, went to the latrine.

Just before he pushed the door open, he was startled by a voice.

"Going somewhere, shitbird?"

It was Sergeant Thomas, fully dressed, complete with his M9 in a leg holster.

"You scared the piss out of me," Minster said.

"Then you don't need to go in there, do you," Thomas replied.

"C'mon, Thomas. You know what I mean."

"That's Sergeant Thomas, Minster. Say Yes, Sergeant."

"Yes, Sergeant Thomas," Minster parroted sarcastically.

"That's enough, Minster. Get in there, do what you have to do, and get back to your bunk," Thomas said sharply.

"I'm awake now, Sergeant Thomas. Getting back in my bunk is not what I want to do."

"If you're that energetic, I can put you on a detail. This hall needs sweeping and mopping."

"You trying to turn this into the army or something?" Minster asked defiantly.

Thomas put his hand on his M9 and in a menacing tone said, "Minster, I've got the okay to shoot you for insubordination. Is that what you want?"

"No, I'll go back to my cot."

"I guess you didn't hear me. I said the hall need sweeping and mopping. The janitor's closet just down the hall has everything you need. Do it right or suffer the consequences."

"Shit," Minster remarked.

"What was that, Minster?"

"I said, sure thing, Sergeant."

"That's what I thought I heard. Now get done with your business and get this hall cleaned."

"Yes, Sergeant Thomas," Minster answered contritely.

Thomas turned and walked off. After taking a few steps, he stopped, turned back toward Minster, and watched him enter the latrine.

As Minster entered the latrine, his only thought was, *I have to get out of this chicken outfit.*

*   *   *

I stood on the porch watching Rahn, Craig, Roop, and Johnson head out. As usual, Johnson was driving. They didn't take a SAW with them, having decided that it was best to leave it behind, just in case. It was the *just in case* that bothered me.

Brian had given them their final briefing at the barn and as far as I knew, he was still there. The creak of the screen door behind me told me someone had come out.

"I guess it's hard watching your children go off to do something dangerous."

Linda.

I didn't have a chance to turn around before she was standing beside me. In the cool night air, I could feel the warmth of her body heat.

"It never gets easy," I answered without looking at her. "Brian went to Iraq when he was still a kid, and my dad went to Vietnam when I was a kid. It isn't easy at all."

Her hand reached over, squeezing between my arm and body. She kept it there with a light hold. "I hope I never have to do that with Ethan or Caleb. I don't think I could stand it."

"I hope you don't, either. It never gets any easier. Craig's my baby, and as I've told him many times, he will always be the baby of the family even when he's sixty." *If he lives that long.*

"You seem so emotionless over it. It doesn't seem to bother you," she said.

"Oh, it bothers me. I stood in the street shouting at Brian when he drove back to Fort Drum that he'd better come home. It bothers me a lot."

"Did he hear you?"

I shrugged. "He told me years later that he did. At the time, I didn't care. I just thought that if I shouted it loud enough he would come back. I guess it worked," I said, the words catching in my throat.

"Yes, I suppose it did. Now you two bicker over your whiskey and cigars," she replied, clearly trying to lighten the mood.

I chuckled, her tactic had worked. "Yeah, of course if he finds them, it will be more than bickering."

I could sense her smiling as she stood there. Sometimes with some people you know when they smile or when they frown or when they are angry with you, even when they don't look it.

"Speaking of whiskey," I said, "would you like to join me for one?"

"I don't think so. I have to get up early with the boys. Donna and I are making extra bandages and some herbal tinctures tomorrow. It sounds like fun, but maybe another time."

"Okay, don't ever say I didn't offer," I replied.

She didn't say anything else. She gave me a hug and went back inside.

The screen door squeaked, announcing her departure without the slam afterward. It was obvious she had held it as it closed.

It was then that I heard someone clear their throat. I knew who it was. "They prepared, Brian?" I asked.

"As best as they can be," he replied as he came up on the porch. "Sorry to interrupt that. It would have been awkward. But if you're offering, I'll share a whiskey with you."

He was another one I could tell when he smiled. As dark as it was, I knew he was smiling one of his shit-eating grins. "Asshole," I muttered.

"What was that?" he asked, the grin still present.

"I said I'll go get it."

"Just tell me where it is and I'll get it."

"You little shit, you were listening, weren't you," I said accusingly.

"Listening to what?" he replied.

"Jerk," I said. "I'll get it; you stay here."

"Maybe a cigar, too, Dad. We could use some bonding time."

"Uh-huh. Bonding time. Okay, just this once, then you're cut off, Mister." I laughed to myself as I went inside for our supplies. That kid had a way about him that was always wheeling and dealing, which is probably why he made such a good intelligence operative.

CHAPTER 10

"The bravest sight in the world is to see a great man struggling against adversity."

—Seneca the Younger

Minster finished sweeping and mopping the hall, mumbling under his breath and twice waking up Major Wolfe with his banging of the mop bucket. He took a little bit of pleasure from knowing Wolfe was pissed but also knowing he was just doing what Sergeant Thomas had told him.

Finishing his task, he put the broom, bucket, and mop back in the janitor's closet. A memory from his short time in the army caused him to stand the mop upward on it's handle to make sure the mop strings were hanging loosely while any wayward strings had been removed or hidden underneath the others. Satisfied that he was finished, Minster headed back toward the assembly hall.

*   *   *

Rahn's team, less Johnson, had been scouting out the armory for almost 24 hours. At 3 a.m., they would begin their movement back toward Johnson and then to the cabin—or Fort Home as Craig had started to call it. That was the magic time. The time when the attention of any sentries was muddy at best and those asleep were in their deepest sleep. It was dark now, and in a few hours, they would begin to withdraw.

Rahn explained this to Roop and then crept back to where Craig was to let him know. Roop and Craig had switched places during the last 8 hours.

"I don't have a watch, First Sergeant," Craig whispered.

"Craig, we have to come to you, so when we come up behind you, then you'll know it's time," Rahn explained.

"I figured that. I'll be ready."

"We'll use the challenge and password. That way, you won't shoot us," Rahn said, smiling. "Just stay alert and know that you'll be back at Fort Home soon."

"Yeah, it keeps Dad from getting mad about calling it the Big House," Craig explained. "I want to come back here for what you're planning."

"You sure? And how do you know what I'm planning?"

"I'm not stupid. It doesn't take a genius to figure out you're coming back. I can handle myself."

"You've proven that. We may need your sniper skills, so I'll talk with Brian and see what he says."

"Roger that, First Sergeant."

"We're gonna make a soldier out of you yet," Rahn said as he placed his hand on Craig's shoulder then crept away in the dark.

He came up on Roop, who was looking through the NVGs. "See anything?" Rahn asked.

"I got movement over by the Conexes. Looks like one guy sneaking around," Roop whispered back.

Rahn held out his hand and Roop placed the NVGs in it. Rahn scanned the area by the Conex, then stopped to focus on one area. "I see him," he said. "One man, he's armed, and it looks like he's going over the hill."

"He's bugging out?" Roop asked.

"Looks like it. We may bring someone back with us—whether he likes it or not," Rahn said, a wicked grin crossing his face. "This might be fun."

Rahn handed the NVGs back to Roop, picked up his weapon and whispered, "Shhh, I'm going hunting."

"Huh?" Roop whispered back.

"I'm gonna catch us some information. Damn, you youngsters can make a guy feel old."

"Okay, First Sergeant," Roop replied, the tone of his voice communicating he still wasn't clear what Rahn was doing.

Creeping through the dark, Rahn's path took him on a course where he would be in front of who he thought was a FEMA member trying to escape. Stopping behind a large scrub bush, he knelt down. He could hear the man approaching as he stumbled through the woods in the darkness.

The man approached Rahn's position and made his way forward. Just as he passed him, Rahn said, "Pssst."

The man stopped instantly, looking around.

"Don't move, asshole," Rahn said firmly.

"Don't shoot. I'm just taking a walk," the man said.

"On your knees, your walk is over," Rahn said as he stood up behind the man.

But as soon as Rahn was on his feet, the man ran. Rahn took off after him.

After a few steps, the man tripped, flying to the ground with a loud "ummph."

Jumping on his back, Rahn pulled out his sheath knife and held it against the man's neck. "Don't move, don't talk," Rahn ordered.

"Okay, okay," the man said.

"I said, don't talk." Rahn pushed the tip of the knife slightly into the man's neck. "Spread your arms out," Rahn directed, picking up the man's M4.

Standing over him, Rahn confirmed he was wearing the black uniform of the FEMA force. "Put your hands behind your back," Rahn ordered.

The man quickly complied.

Removing a pair of zip handcuffs from his pocket, Rahn quickly put them on the man.

"Roll over," Rahn said, and again the man complied. His thin face was eerily skeletal-looking in the darkness with only a sliver of moon to provide any light. His eyes grew wide as he saw Rahn's camouflaged face over him.

"Don't hurt me," he whined.

"I said, don't talk," Rahn said menacingly as he jabbed the barrel of his weapon into the man's chest. Sitting on him, Rahn removed a small roll of duct tape, tore off a strip, and put it over the man's mouth.

Then, getting off the man, he reached down and grabbed the man's shirt, pulling on it, Rahn helped the man stand. Turning the man so he faced north toward where Craig was, he poked him in the back with his weapon and said, "Start walking."

After about ten minutes, Rahn said, "Stop."

Peering into the darkness, he whispered, "Pinball." It was the challenge word he had told Craig earlier. Waiting a few seconds, he again said, "Pinball."

This time a whispered response came in the darkness. "Stadium."

"It's me," Rahn said slightly louder than a whisper. "I have a guest." They proceeded to walk toward Craig.

Craig was kneeling behind a large hemlock, his weapon pointing toward Rahn and the guest. "What the hell," Craig remarked. "What is this?"

"I caught this boy sneaking away from the armory," Rahn answered.

"Why didn't you just kill him?" Craig asked.

Hearing these words, the man slumped as his knees seemed to weaken.

"They'd have found the body and known somebody was here."

"So, we'll kill him later," Craig said.

This caused the man to fall to the ground.

"Not yet, maybe later. We need information and this runner will give it to us. What he says will determine if he lives or dies. We'll take him back with us and question him there."

Craig nodded in understanding.

"Keep an eye on him. I'm going to get our partner." Rahn knew better than to use names. "Then, we'll head back. If he runs, use that knife your brother gave you."

Keeping his focus on the man, Craig thought back to just before they had departed. Brian had come up to him and handed him a USMC issue Ka-Bar. It had a 7-inch blade that Brian kept sharply honed.

"Dad gave me this before I went to Iraq. He said he had it for almost his entire army career, even took it to Central America with him."

"Dad was in Central America?" Craig asked.

"Yeah, but he never said what he was doing there. Anyway, he told me it had a rule."

"What's the rule?" Craig asked.

"Draw me without honor, sheath me without blood."

"Did you use it over there?"

"Yes," Brian answered with a far off look he sometimes got. "I didn't break any rules."

Rahn returned a few minutes later, with Roop bringing up the rear. "Let's get out of Dodge," he ordered.

As the prisoner walked by him, Craig reached out and sliced the man on the shoulder, a small trickle of blood forming.

The man tried to scream out, but the tape prevented anything but a slight sound.

Rahn gave Craig a "what the hell are you doing" look.

Wiping the blade on the man's shirt, Craig said, "Not breaking any rules today, First Sergeant."

The four men headed into the darkness.

*   *   *

I was standing on the porch watching Mike, Ethan, and Caleb creeping around the edge of the woods beside the house. Mike had his .22, and they were looking for squirrels and rabbits. This close to the house, I think the rodents had pretty well become extinct as Mike was a good shot.

The two younger boys enjoyed being with Mike, and he liked playing the role of a big brother. They would stop every now and then, and Mike would have all of them kneel as they searched the brush and tree branches for anything living.

I smiled at first; this was the new way kids played. Not unlike how we played when I was a kid—only we didn't always play with real weapons.

I was a little sad because this was also how these boys would develop the skills to become the warriors they needed to become later. At nine, Mike wasn't much younger than Rick, who was already so different from the way he arrived here a few months ago. He had even taken to spending time in the bunker with Craig, Allen, and Sajan when they were on guard. That occasionally created issues as the two younger boys wanted to hang out there as well, but they were much too young.

The younger boy of the two—Caleb—was the real challenge. He was an independent little shit and had to be stopped a couple of times physically, kicking and shouting that he wanted to go, too. Linda had her hands full with that one.

The creak of the screen door behind me told me someone had come outside. A few seconds later, a hand lightly touched my lower back and a voice said, "Have they found anything yet?" It was Linda. She removed her hand and came to stand alongside me.

We both stood there and watched the boys continue their search. They'd walk a few steps, Mike would raise his fist slightly in the air, and they would all kneel down. The National Guard guys had been teaching him patrol hand signals and he was a quick study. Much to Nancy's dismay, he was also a quick study at learning the soldiers' lingo. I had bar soap and told her how I had used it on Brian when he was a kid. She took to the suggestion.

"I don't think there are any rabbits or squirrels anywhere near the cabin anymore," I said.

A sharp *crack* sounded in the air as Mike shot his .22. I saw Ethan take off running into the brush. Before I could shout for him to stop, he bent over and proudly raised a cottontail up by its ears.

"You got him, Mike," he shouted. The three boys jumped up and down in their excitement.

"Who's going to gut him and skin him?" Linda shouted. A bit of laughter was in her voice.

"I will, Momma," Ethan shouted back.

"I guess there was one hold out in the brush," I said, chuckling.

"They are turning into good hunters. Do you have any more .22s?" she asked. "Ethan will be asking for one soon."

"I have three more in the gun safe. I always figured we'd do most of our hunting with them, if it came to that."

"What about deer, turkey, you know, the good stuff?" she said.

"There will be time for that, too."

"I'm a pretty good deer hunter. I got a six-pointer two years ago— That seems like a long time ago now, as if it almost didn't happen."

"I know the feeling. Everything has changed, and I can't say it's all been for the worst."

"How can you say that, John? Especially after all of this. My boys are innocent and—"

I cut her off. "I'm not talking about the deaths and the violence. I'm talking about how things have become. How what was important before doesn't matter anymore."

"I don't understand," she said.

"Before the EMP, well, even before I moved up here, I chased the dollar. What was important to me was to make money to buy a better quality of life for my family, for myself. I wanted the toys and I wanted the stuff. Then, I won the lottery and I had it all. Suddenly, working hard stopped and didn't matter. So, I came up here to get a small cabin and some peace."

"This isn't a small cabin, John. I've said that before."

"No, I suppose it isn't. When Brian and his family got here and the EMP happened, things started to change. What was *important* started to change. I brought Craig and Donna up here, and Carol moved in, then the others. What was important has continued to change. It's no longer about work, work, work. It's about relationships. It's about friends and family. Friends became family. You're part of that family now, too."

"Ha," she laughed. "It's a pretty weird family." And she laughed some more. "I'm not being mean, I'm just saying it's a weird group that has come together. A fun kind of weird in the middle of all this ugliness."

"It is that," I chuckled. "We still work hard, but we make time for each other. We don't hide in our work." Then, pausing and raising an eyebrow like Mr. Spock of the old Star Trek TV series, I added, "Some of us still hide in that work. Some of us have people right here who would gladly be good friends, but there seems to be a resistance."

"You talking about me?"

"Well, if the shoe fits," I said sarcastically. "You do seem to do almost nothing but work. It would be nice to see you join in more when we're having fun. I've asked you several times to sit and talk. You always have work to do."

"Work is important."

"I won't deny that, Linda. So are friends and real relationships. I had an acquaintance back before all of this who had hundreds of friends on social media. Her husband was always telling her to get out, have real friends; those technology friends were just imaginary. Oh, they would fight over that. She had an e-commerce business and made good money. Finally, her husband divorced her and her kids went to live with their dad because she never spent *real time* with them. She was all alone. Real friends are what matters. We have time for that now and we should take care of those friendships."

"I have friends," she said a bit testily, letting go of my hand.

"Is that why you left Chilton or Hilbert or wherever you came from?" I regretted the words as soon as I said them. It was mean of me.

"I came here to find family," she shot back. If anything, Linda could stand her ground.

"I'm saying that in our new world, the way we were before no longer matters. What matters now is friends, family, and the relationships we have with each other. Working and making money doesn't matter anymore. What's important is having relationships that can help us all get through this together. People that will be there for us. Do what they say, keep their word and support us, even when we act like we don't want them around."

"I suppose," she said, "but I still don't like it. I have things to do; I'll chat with you later."

She started to turn away and I said, "Linda, please just listen to what I said. Think it over."

"I heard you, John," she remarked and walked away.

"Hearing and listening are two different things," I said under my breath.

CHAPTER 11

"You can't find that which does not wish to be found."

—Nancy Henry

"Major Wolfe," said a man's voice.

Major Elias Wolfe looked up from the papers he was reading at his desk. Platoon Sergeant Mark Thomas stood in the doorway. "What is it, Sergeant?" Wolfe asked.

"We have a situation, sir," Thomas answered.

"Well, come in, Sergeant," Wolfe said testily. "I don't have all day."

"At roll call this morning one of the men was missing. So was his gear. Looks like he went AWOL."

"WHO?" Wolfe shouted, rising behind his desk.

"It's Minster, sir. Apparently, he left sometime in the middle of the night."

"How in the hell did this happen," Wolfe shouted. "Who was on guard?"

"I have them waiting in the assembly hall. They said they didn't see anything."

"Were they sleeping? I won't tolerate that. Take me to them," he said, walking rapidly out the door and heading down the hall. Thomas followed at almost a jog.

"I'll have somebody shot," Wolfe roared as he turned down the hallway. As he entered the hall, six men stood off to the side, the other men standing in a formation, their eyes going from the six men to the major and back toward the men again.

Stopping in front of the six men, Wolfe said to Thomas, "Are these the guards from last night?"

"Yes sir, these are the men."

"What the hell happened?" Wolfe demanded.

The men stood quietly, each looking downward. The silence in the hall was deafening.

"I asked a question. What the hell happened?" Wolfe demanded.

"Sir, we didn't see anything," one of the guards spoke.

"You were on guard. You are responsible," Wolfe shouted. Saliva dripped from his mouth and sprayed as he shouted. "Somebody wasn't doing their god-damned job."

"We were doing what we were supposed to be, Major," the man said. "We didn't see anything."

Wolfe's eyes scanned all six men. His hands on his hips, he started to rock back and forth, a vein popping out in his neck. "Somebody was derelict. Somebody should have seen something. No one goes AWOL. NO ONE!"

The men stood there silently.

"Sir, we didn't see anything. Not a thing…last night," the man repeated.

"Major, should I send a patrol out, try and find him, and bring him back?" Thomas asked.

"Yes, goddammit. Send out *two* patrols. I want that son of a bitch here and I want him now.

"Yes, sir. I'll send them out immediately," Thomas replied. "You six, come with me. Grab your shit and let's go."

The six men didn't waste any time. Each ran and got their vests and weapons, quickly following Thomas as he left the hall.

Wolfe went over to the formation and stared at the men standing there. "No one," he said. "No *one* goes AWOL. When we find Minster, he will be brought back here and shot. Am I clear?"

"Yes, sir," the men said.

"I said, am I clear?" Wolfe shouted.

"Yes, Sir," the men shouted back at him.

Spinning on his heels, Wolfe stormed out of the assembly hall.

I'll shoot that son of a bitch myself.

*   *   *

The sun was still low in the eastern sky as Rahn and his team drove onto the acreage that surrounded the cabin area.

Brian and I were on the porch enjoying a second cup of morning coffee as they arrived. It appeared Specialist Johnson was driving, Roop in the turret. Johnson headed straight for the barn.

As they drove by, I saw Craig sitting in the back with another person.

What the hell?

We got up and left our coffee on the porch as we headed toward the barn.

"Looks like an extra person," Brian commented.

"Yeah, and there better be a good reason for it," I replied.

We wasted no time getting to the barn. Craig was coming out of the back of the Humvee, his weapon pointing at the extra person.

"Out, dickweed," I heard him say as we got closer.

Rahn had also gotten out and was heading toward us as Roop came out of the turret.

A man clad in a black uniform stumbled out of the vehicle, his hands behind his back. It took a minute before I realized he was restrained in flex-cuffs. He was also blindfolded. I was pretty certain he was not visiting because he wanted to.

"What's up, First Sergeant?" Brian asked.

Surprisingly, Rahn saluted him. That kind of military custom had not been used much here.

Brian saluted back, the smirk on his face showed he was intrigued, too.

As I got closer, I saw the FEMA patch on the black uniform and figured it had something to do with their guest. I decided, and unusually so, to not ask anything and let the soldiers do what they had to do.

"Who do we have here?" Brian asked, pointing at the FEMA guy.

"Caught him trying to sneak out of the armory. Tough boy here was going AWOL," Rahn said.

"Well, well, well. A deserter. I wonder why," Brian replied.

The FEMA guy tried to speak but the duct tape on his mouth prevented everything but mumbled and unintelligible sounds.

"Whatchya gonna do with him?" Brian asked. His tone was stern and were it not for his smirk, I'd think he meant something very different than what he was trying to say.

"He's going to tell us everything he knows," Rahn explained.

Approaching the FEMA captive, Rahn grabbed the man's biceps tightly and said, "Aren't ya? You're going to tell us everything you know."

The man struggled a bit and tried to pull away.

Rahn tightened his grip, and Craig put the muzzle of his AR against the guy's face. He calmed down quickly then.

"Where are you going to keep him?" Brian asked.

"I figured in one of the stalls in the barn. We can chain him up; some of our guys are in there to keep an eye on him, too."

"Do what you do best, First Sergeant," Brian said.

Rahn called for Johnson and Roop. "Take this boy into the barn, get him comfortable, and chain him up. We'll come visit him in a bit."

"Roger, First Sergeant," the two responded at the same time. Johnson and Roop each grabbed an arm on the man and marched him into the barn.

"How did that happen?" Brian asked.

We saw him early this morning sneaking out of the armory and heading for the woods. I intercepted him. He said he was taking a walk."

"Not the most original excuse I ever heard," Brian said. "Has he said any more?"

"The nametag on his uniform says his name is Minster. I took his wallet and the ID inside said his name is Corey Minster. Local boy, too."

"How local?" I asked, finally entering the conversation.

"Oh, hi Dad," Brian said. "You just getting here? I thought you were on the porch, it was so quiet."

"Screw you, Brian," I said. "How local is he, Chris?"

"He's from Suamico?"

"Where's that?" Brian asked.

"Oh, that's right. You aren't from around here, are you?" I said in a fake hillbilly accent. "It's near Green Bay."

"That ain't too local. It's good information, though. I wonder how many of those FEMA boys are cheeseheads?" Brian asked.

"We're going to find out. And a whole lot more," Rahn said. His tone was ominous.

I had to ask, "How are you going to get that information?"

"Enhanced interrogation," Rahn replied. "He'll tell us one way or another."

I gave Rahn a pointed look. "You gotta remember we have kids here. They can't be around that kind of thing."

"Good point," Brian answered. "We'll take him over to the Quints' old place. There are still out buildings over there."

"Just keep him away from the kids is all I ask. Other than that, you can shoot the son of a bitch for all I care." I felt raw hate climbing up my neck. The images of what had happened at the Winstons' place was still fresh in my mind. Their daughter, Emma, was still traumatized, and she didn't need to see this guy, either. We had asked her to start sitting on the porch with us during our meetings, and sometimes, Linda or Donna would sit alone with her. I was glad she'd been inside when they arrived and took him out of the vehicle. She still reacted when she saw our HMMWVs. The black one that we had repaired and got running really set her off. So much so, that we had started keeping her inside when we knew it would be used. No one wanted her to have a set back, and I was pretty certain a black-clad FEMA guy would do that.

Craig walked up and handed Brian a Ka-bar. "Here, Bri," he said. "I kept the rules. You can have this back now."

I recognized the knife. It was the same one I had given Brian before he went to Iraq, the same one I had used in Nicaragua and Honduras. It was also the knife Brian had used in the field against the bikers when we rescued Mike.

"Keep it. It's yours now," Brian said.

Craig was obviously taken aback, but he smiled and said, "Thank you." Then, he quickly put the scabbard back on his belt.

"What rules?" I asked.

"The one you told me, Dad. Draw me without honor…" Brian answered.

I glanced at Craig and wondered how he'd kept the rules. I decided if he wanted me to know, he'd tell me. That would be hard for me to keep to, but I needed to. Dads can't know everything.

"Craig!" a loud, young female voice shouted. It caused all of us to turn and look at the growing row of cabins we had built. Addie was running toward us with her arms outstretched.

Craig almost dropped everything as he fumbled to quickly fix his belt and head toward her.

"The love birds reunited," Brian said.

"Kinda reminds me of those old commercials where the man and woman are running toward each other in a field," Rahn quipped.

"You two leave 'em alone," I said. "At least someone around here is happy." *I hope we don't have any surprises coming from those two. Gary said he thinks they've been busy like bunnies.*

A scream behind us got our attention and we all turned around. Donna and Linda had brought Emma outside and were heading toward the garden. Emma's blood-curdling scream had made everyone jump.

As the two of them tried to get her back into the cabin, her screaming shouts of "He's one of them, he's one of them," were ear-shattering.

"Fuck," I shouted as I ran toward the trio and helped get her back inside. "Why is she out here?" I demanded.

Nearly in tears, Linda explained, "We thought seeing the garden might help her, to see what we were doing here."

"Obviously, that didn't work," I said, not too kindly.

"We didn't know you had a visitor," Donna said sharply.

Emma had seen the prisoner. I didn't know if he was someone that was actually at the Winstons' farm or if it was the black uniform he was wearing, but the damage was done.

Rahn shouted, "Get him in the barn. NOW!"

This was not good.

*   *   *

The two search teams had been looking all over Antigo and the surrounding areas. Thinking Minster was stupid enough to head toward Wausau or even west toward Rhinelander, the two HMMWVs took different paths. One team went south on Highway 45 and the other went west on Highway 64.

The southbound team turned onto side streets looking between houses, at businesses, and anywhere they thought Minster might be hiding. They even checked the funeral home and each of the parks as they headed south.

The westbound team did the same. Neither team thought they'd actually find the man, unless he was stupid enough to be walking along the road.

Back at the armory, Wolfe and Thomas were in his office looking at the map of Eastern Langlade

County, focusing on the area from the Evergreen State Fish Hatchery to Markton.

"He's somewhere in this area," Wolfe said, pointing at the area east of the hatchery.

"He couldn't have walked that far, sir," Thomas remarked.

"What? Who, dammit, Thomas? I'm not talking about our runner. I'm talking about Henry and Rahn. They are somewhere in this area."

"Sorry, sir. I was momentarily confused," Thomas said.

"Well, get your head out of your ass and pay attention. They're somewhere here is where they are, and I need to find them."

"Should we send out more scout teams, sir?"

"We will soon, but they're going to be both mobile and on foot. We aren't going to find anything driving around on the roads, looking at the trees passing by."

"These men aren't all that skilled, sir. Just a few of us have military training. Some of these guys were prison guards and they don't walk much."

"They're going to have to, Thomas. You'll lead a patrol out here," Wolfe said, pointing at the area surrounding where the town of Lake View had been. "We'll set up here, near the hatchery, and use that as an advanced CP."

"Sir, I was in the air force. I don't know army acronyms. What's a CP?"

"CP, Sergeant Thomas, is a command post. It will be the base camp for our patrols. You do know what a base camp is?" Wolfe quipped in a condescending tone.

"Yes, sir."

"Good, we're making progress then. Now, we'll take a dozen men there. A couple of field tents and vehicles to support them, plus a fuel bladder. We'll send them out on foot and they can reconnoiter the area. Where was that farmhouse that Jamison was killed at?"

"Here, sir," Thomas said, pointing at an area to the north and west of Lake View.

"I'm almost tempted to set up there. Symbolism is everything sometimes, but it might be too risky. Henry probably would figure that out."

"I think the hatchery's a good idea, sir. It's close enough to not waste time and far enough away to make it an effort to get to us."

"Exactly, Sergeant Thomas. So, this is what we'll do…"

CHAPTER 12

"The greatest mistake you can make in life is to continually fear that you will make one."

—Elbert Hubbard

It was after dark when they moved the man—Minster, as they now called him, to the barn at Quint's old place. When they'd first put him in the stall at the Henrys's, they had stripped him, chained him to a ceiling beam, and left him there. Rahn wasn't about to let him have any comforts.

After the scene outside the barn earlier, Rahn wanted to know exactly what this guy knew and if he was at the massacre. It had taken Donna and Linda hours to calm Emma down, and afterward, the women were an emotional mess. Between anger and shock over what had happened, they had distanced themselves from everyone.

Now, Minster was chained to a beam in the barn on Quint's farm, his toes barely touching the ground, and Rahn, Johnson, Brian, and Roop stood watching. Rahn had an old shovel handle in his hand and was slapping it in the palm of his other hand as Minster stared in horror at him.

Brian went out to the well, filled a bucket with water, and came back inside. "This will get his attention," he said.

Tossing the water onto Minster, the man shuddered from the coldness of it.

"You're going to tell us everything you know," Rahn said as he continued to slap the handle in his hand.

"I don't know anything," Minster cried, his teeth chattering. He was cold due to the cold water, his nakedness, and the cool night air.

"I think you do," Rahn said.

Roop and Johnson shuffled their feet on the floor of the barn.

Rahn turned to them both, and in a low voice said, "This might get real ugly. If you can't handle it, leave now. I can't have you interrupting us."

"I'm fine, First Sergeant," Johnson said.

"I think I need some fresh air. I'll go outside for a bit," Roop added.

"Go ahead, soldier," Rahn said. "No shame in leaving. This isn't for everyone."

Roop turned and walked out of the barn. He stopped outside the door, the light from a kerosene lantern shining beyond the door and turning the ground yellow. A loud SMACK and a howl of pain followed him out.

*　　　*　　　*

Waking early, Wolfe went to the communications room. He wanted to contact Rick Barstow, the FEMA Regional Administrator.

Entering the room, he pointed at an idle radio operator and said, "You, get me Wausau. I want to talk to Rick Barstow."

"Yesss sir," the operator replied nervously. Grabbing the radio handset, he depressed the PTT button and said, "Wausau Base, Wausau Base. This is Antigo Base, over."

After a brief delay, he heard, "Antigo Base, this is Wausau Base, over."

"Wausau Base. Request Wausau 6 for Antigo 6, over."

"Antigo Base, stand by."

Putting his hand over the mic, the operator said, "They probably have to go and find him, Major."

Wolfe folded his arms across his chest and nodded. *They probably had to wake him up. May be curled up with one of the cooperative lady refugees.*

While he waited, he observed the other operators. They seemed to all be doing something but whether or not it required three of them to do it, he wondered.

He would need a forward operator with the deployment of teams to the hatchery and then one back here. *That third one can probably start working again and do it forward of here.*

"Antigo Base, this is Wausau Base, we have Wausau 6, over," the metallic voice surprised him as it came through the speaker.

The operator stood up from his chair and motioned for Wolfe to take his place. He then slid the microphone closer to Wolfe and showed him where the PTT button was.

"I know where it is," Wolfe said sharply. Taking the microphone, Wolfe pressed the button. "Wausau 6, this is Antigo 6, over."

"That you, Wolfe?" the voice over the radio said.

Shaking his head and muttering the word idiot, Wolfe replied, "Wausau 6, I'm requesting supplies, over."

"What do you need, Wolfe?" Barstow asked.

Dammit, I wish he'd use proper radio procedure.

"Wausau 6, this is Antigo 6. I need a couple of fuel bladders, full, 5,000 rounds of 5.56, 2,500 rounds of 7.62, a general purpose large tent, a general purpose small tent, and 20 cases of MREs, over."

"Anything else, a hot tub, golf clubs? What the hell are you doing up there, Wolfe?"

"Wausau 6, this is Antigo 6, taking the fight to the enemy, over."

"What have you been doing? I sent you up there for a reason. If you aren't capable of doing the mission, I'll find someone else."

Wolfe could feel his temper rising. Taking a deep breath to calm himself, he replied, "Wausau 6, I need these supplies to accomplish this mission, over."

"When?"

"Wausau 6, as soon as possible, over."

"I'll be in touch."

Wolfe sat and waited. Not hearing anymore, he called, "Wausau 6, this is Antigo 6, over."

"Antigo 6, this is Wausau Base. Wausau 6 has left the area, over."

"Wausau Base, this is Antigo 6, out," Wolfe answered. *Dammit. He better get me those supplies.*

* * *

I was eating breakfast in the kitchen when I heard the back door open. The heavy tread of several pairs of boots told me it was more than one person. I looked up, holding some oatmeal on my spoon as Rahn and Brian entered. They looked tired. Rahn was wet as if he'd poured water over himself.

"You two finish your business?" I asked.

I guess my tone was less than supportive. I knew we needed the information. Without it, we only had a small part of the picture. I wasn't sure I could completely agree with what they had done, even after what I witnessed at the Winstons.

"Yeah, Dad, we got it," Brian answered. He walked over to the stove, grabbed two cups off of the counter, and taking the old school coffee percolator off the stove, poured two cups. He walked back over and gave a cup to Rahn.

"I don't get one," I said.

"You have one," he replied.

Rahn snorted in his coffee.

I glared at both of them. Getting up, I went to the stove, grabbed the pot and poured myself another cup. Then, set the pot back on the stove, walked to my chair and sat down. "What did you get?"

"Our buddy Wolfe is back and is in charge. He brought reinforcements with him, too, about 30 men. They have 7 HMMWVs, a 5-ton, and one automatic weapon. Minster, the guy's name is Corey Minster, said it was an M60."

"An M60, they still have those?" I asked.

"We had them in Iraq and some regular units still have a couple around," Brian said.

"So a light machine gun, 7.62 caliber with an effective range of 1,000 meters," I said.

"Not bad, old man," Brian said, grinning. "This one is mounted on one of their Hummers."

"That's all you got?" I asked. "You beat a man all night and that's all you got."

"We didn't beat him all night, John," Rahn said defensively.

"We waterboarded him, too, Dad," Brian said. He wasn't smiling this time. "No, we got names, who's in charge, and who their lower-level leaders are. I have the name of another guy that was at the Winstons. His name is Edmiston."

I'll remember that name.

Leaning back in my chair, I asked, "And what did your patrol give you?"

"We know their security is lax; this guy snuck out right between two guards. We counted the vehicles, we know they are bunked in the assembly hall, and we know they have local civilians doing all the dirty work for them. According to Minster, some of the FEMA guys are amusing themselves with a few local women."

"And what is Minster's status?" I asked.

"He was at the Winstons's place, too. He said he didn't want to, but they made him assault the woman," Rahn said.

"You believe him?" I said, looking at Rahn squarely.

"Nope," Rahn said.

I turned my attention to Brian. "So what next?"

"We'll execute him for rape and murder," Brian said.

"Yeah? Who's going to do that?" I asked, somewhat stunned.

"I am," Rahn and Brian said simultaneously.

*   *   *

"What?" Craig asked as he sat upright in bed. "Are you serious?"

He was in Addie's cabin, spread out on the rope bed with Addie. They had made several rope beds for the cabins.

"Yes, I am," Addie said, a guarded tone in her voice.

"Wow," Craig exclaimed with an exhale. "I'm gonna be a dad."

Saying the words aloud seemed to make it more real, and a grin spread across his face that morphed into a full-blown ear to ear smile. "I'm gonna be a father."

He reached for Addie and pulled her to him for a long embrace. It was then he noticed she was crying.

"What's wrong?" he asked, gently brushing her hair away from her eyes.

"I was afraid," she said quietly.

"Afraid? Of what?"

"Afraid you'd be mad."

"Oh, Addie. I'm not mad, I'm excited," he said with reserved enthusiasm. "Wow."

He hugged her again as once more, his face-splitting grin appeared. "Of course, we'll have to get married."

Addie stiffened in his arms, enough that Craig, in his enthusiasm noticed. "You don't have to marry me, Craig."

"Of course I do," he replied. "My son will have married parents."

"And if it's a girl?" Addie shot back.

"Then, *she'll* have married parents," Craig said.

"You have all the answers, don't you," she remarked with a hint of sarcasm.

"I'm a Henry. Of course, I do," Craig said. Then, catching himself, he added, "And you will be, too, so you'll be just as smart as the rest of us."

The comment made Addie laugh, which made Craig feel much better about everything.

"I'm still scared," she said. "Having a baby out here isn't that simple. What if there's a problem? What if something bad happens?" Her voice caught slightly.

"My mom is here; she knows about this stuff. Linda will help, too. You'll be fine, my sweet Addie. It will all be fine." He took her hand in his. "Will you marry me?"

She finally smiled at him. "Yes. Yes, I will."

CHAPTER 13

*"The world breaks every one and afterward
many are strong at the broken places."*

—Ernest Hemingway

"Antigo 6, Antigo 6, this is Wausau Base, over."

"Wausau Base, this is Antigo Base, over."

"Antigo Base, Wausau 6 wants Antigo 6, over."

"Wait one moment, over." The radio operator got up from his chair, raced out of the communications room and down the hall. Knocking on the door, he waited.

Major Wolfe looked up at the man and said, "Yes, what is it?"

"Sir, Wausau 6 is on the radio. He wants to speak with you directly."

"On my way," Wolfe said as he rose from his desk and followed the operator down the hall.

Sitting back in his chair, the operator picked up the microphone and said, "Wausau Base, I have Antigo 6, over." He then handed the microphone to Major Wolfe.

Taking the mic, Wolfe stared at the operator, who immediately gave his chair to Wolfe. "Wausau Base, this is Antigo 6, over."

"Antigo 6, this is Wausau Base, stand by, over."

"I thought you said he wanted to speak with me?" an exasperated Wolfe said.

"That's what they said, Major," the operator replied.

A few minutes went by before a voice on the radio said, "Elias, this is Barstow."

When will this man learn proper radio procedure? "Wausau 6, this is Antigo 6, over," Wolfe said.

"Elias, you're getting one bladder with five hundred gallons, the tentage, ammunition, and MREs you asked for. It's all I can do for now," Barstow said.

"Wausau 6, this is Antigo 6, when will it be arriving, over."

"Tomorrow. The men and vehicle will return here, am I clear?"

"Wausau 6, Roger," Wolfe replied. *Damn, I was going to try and keep them, too.*

"Antigo 6, this is Wausau Base, out."

And the transmission ended.

"Well, that's better than nothing," Wolfe remarked more to himself than anyone else.

He rose and left the room, heading down the armory hall toward the assembly hall where he hoped to find Thomas. He no sooner entered the large gymnasium-like area when he heard, "Hello Major, I was just coming to see you."

It was Thomas, and he had the four guards with him who had been out looking for Minster.

"Sergeant Thomas," he replied. "These men find that runaway filth?"

"No, sir, we didn't," one of the men spoke. "We looked everywhere we could think of, Major. We didn't see anything of him anywhere."

Wolfe glared at the man for a moment and then said, "Very well, you men are dismissed. Sergeant, a word."

The four men looked at each other in surprise and then quickly left the area, heading out of the assembly hall.

"Yes, sir," Thomas said.

"We have supplies coming tomorrow. I want you to pick four two-man teams and four HM-

MWVs. Pick one of the radio operators, too. We're going to the hatchery to set up a Forward Operating Base. We will operate from there for a while."

"Yes sir, that's the plan we discussed before, correct?"

"Yes, it is."

"What equipment did you get, Major? Are we getting everything?"

"Pretty much. We aren't getting all of the fuel I wanted, but I didn't exactly tell them how much I needed. I think 500 gallons is enough, don't you?" Wolfe answered with a glint in his eyes. *Five hundred gallons isn't close to enough, but I'll take what I can get.*

"Even all the ammo, sir?"

"Yup. Of course, the FOB teams will be living off of MREs, but that should keep them motivated to complete the mission faster."

"Yes, sir."

"Make it happen, Thomas. I'll be going with them. I want you to stay here and keep these people on their toes. If necessary, we'll rotate ourselves out after five days. I don't think it will take that long."

"I thought you wanted me to go with them, Major?"

"I did, but I need you to keep training these people. They need it."

"Yes sir, I'm on it," Thomas replied as he saluted.

Wolfe returned the salute and headed back to his office.

*   *   *

"John," Sam said as he approached me near the gardens. I was looking at all of the vegetables we had coming in and how timing had been on our side with expanding the garden. We had several different kinds of beans, cucumbers, tomatoes, hot and bell peppers, spinach, onions, garlic, potatoes, corn, carrots, and lettuce. That was just the vegetables. Donna and Linda had a large herb garden we used for cooking and medicinal purposes. I had no idea what was in that and left them to it.

I must have been really studying the garden as Sam had to repeat himself, "John," which caused me to jump slightly.

"What's up, Sam?" I asked.

"Wolfe has been at it again. He has supplies coming, tents, ammo, fuel, and food. He said something about taking the fight to the enemy."

"Hmm… He must be sending people out to stay for a while. With the tents, it sounds like he's going to establish what Brian calls a FOB."

"A FOB, John," Sam said.

"Yup, FOB, Forward Operating Base. It's funny, but Brian told me the guys to man the FOBs who never left them are called Fobbits. Tolkein strikes again."

"We called them REMFs," Sam said, chuckling. "Their language today, often cruder than ours, is also better suited for a more diverse military."

"We were diverse, Sam."

"I meant more women. Can you imagine a woman being called a REMF or calling someone that?"

"What's a REMF?" a female voice asked.

Sam and I had been so engrossed in our conversation that we hadn't heard Linda come up behind us.

"Oh, hi, Linda, we didn't hear you walk up," I said.

"So, what's a REMF?" she repeated.

"I'll let you explain that one, John," Sam said with a smile as he walked away, leaving Linda and me by the garden.

"Is it that bad?" Linda said. "It's not like I haven't heard cussing before and I can cuss with the best of them."

"It's not bad. We were talking about how soldiers refer to those in the rear. Those not in a combat area. When Sam was in the navy during Vietnam there was a rather nasty expression that the grunts—the infantry guys—used to describe anyone that wasn't like them."

"Like them?" she asked, raising her brows.

"Yeah, guys out in the front lines searching for the enemy and shooting and getting shot at daily. Like that."

"Okay."

"So the term was, Rear Echelon, Mother—, you know," I explained. I usually had a hard time with that word around women, not always but sometimes. "They just shortened it to REMF and pronounced it as its spelled."

"What do they call them today?"

"According to Brian and Rahn, they call them fobbits or POGs."

"I don't get it. What does that mean?"

"A fobbit is someone who goes to a Forward Operating Base, they call those FOBs, and stays on the base. They never go outside the perimeter. A

POG is an acronym for People Other than Grunts. Grunts are the infantry."

"You guys have the strangest language," she said. Pausing for a second, she began again. "Who was that guy in the black uniform yesterday?"

"He was a FEMA guy that Rahn captured when they scouted the armory. Apparently, he was trying to run away and they caught him."

"Was that smart?"

"What, trying to run away or getting caught and being brought here?" I replied humorously.

"I'm trying to be serious here, John. Don't be a jerk about it."

"Sorry." For some reason, I had found myself apologizing to Linda a lot more often lately. More than anyone I knew, it seemed. "They needed information, so bringing him here for interrogation was important."

"But Emma saw him; you saw what happened."

"They didn't know Emma would be out. They were putting him in the barn. They ended up taking him over to Quint's old barn."

"Who's Quint?"

"Rick's grandfather. The next place over was his, where we got all the doors and windows for the cabins. Quint was killed when a looter band tried to attack us. They also killed Addie's parents and, well, uh…"

"Addie told me, I know," Linda said softly. "So, what did this guy tell you?"

"He was one of them. He was among the men who attacked the Winstons, killed everyone and assaulted Sarah."

Linda put her hand up to her mouth, the shock on her face very clear. "He was?"

"Yes, he said he was made to do it, but he was there. He actively participated in it."

"Why would he tell you that? Why would he confess to something like that?" she asked, clearly shocked.

"Rahn and Brian encouraged him."

"What does that mean?" she asked vehemently.

I looked directly at her, then scrunched my mouth together while closing my eyes. I shrugged.

"You tortured him," she said accusingly.

"I *didn't* torture him."

"Don't play word games, John; you know what I meant. They tortured him. I can't get my head around that. I mean, the man is garbage, but torture? I thought we were better than that."

"It's a tough and ugly new world, Linda. If it helps, Rahn said it didn't really take a lot for the guy to tell everything. Seems the threat was as powerful as doing it."

"Still, we are better than that," she said, pointing her finger into my chest.

I stood there silently as she stomped away. She was mad. She was right but so were we. It *is* a tough and ugly new world and I was afraid it was going to get a lot uglier.

Watching her as she entered the cabin, I suddenly remembered Sam was explaining what Wolfe and FEMA were up to when she showed up. I took off for the barn to hear Sam's news.

Arriving in his radio room slightly out of breath, I put my hands on my thighs and leaned over. The deep gasps I was making caused Sam to chuckle.

"You're getting old, John," he remarked.

"I'm not old," I replied. "I'm not used to running."

"That's your lie, John, you tell it," he said with a laugh.

"So what is FEMA up to," I asked, having caught my breath.

"They have supplies coming; a fuel bladder, tents, ammo, and rations," he explained."That could be just for resupply," I said.

"It could, but why the tents? They have the armory. Rahn said you could billet over 120 men in there with ease. The tents suggest something else."

"Like a forward base or something?" I asked.

"Could be," Sam replied.

"I need to find Jake. I have a mission for his boys—see if they can find that base."

"They're still at the armory. The stuff doesn't arrive until tomorrow. I figure if it is a base, they won't move out until the day after."

"That's even better. We can position Jake's boys along 64. A good place would be near Four Corners. Only two ways they can go from there. We put another team near the fish hatchery on P and another team a little further east in case they take one of those roads east of Four Corners."

I had just finished when a pounding of feet on the steps coming up to Sam's area got our attention.

"Mr. Henry, Mr. Henry, you need to come to the cabin now. Something bad has happened." It was Sajan. Because he was normally pretty leveled headed, I knew it was serious.

Following him, I asked, "What's wrong?"

His reply stopped me cold on the steps. "The girl, the one you brought back. She's dead. She killed herself."

CHAPTER 14

*"He who does not punish evil commands
it to be done."*

—Leonardo da Vinci

We had the funeral the next day. There was some discussion regarding where to bury Emma Winston. Some felt she belonged with her family, but when I explained that we had cremated the family those opinions changed. It was decided we'd bury her in our yet small—but we were certain it was going to grow—cemetery at the back of the meadow. There, she would rest with Carol and Grady.

It was a simple ceremony and not many of us attended. We hardly knew her. I had never seen her until we rescued her. I just knew she existed.

Linda and Donna each said a few words. It was a sad testimony to a life taken too soon.

*   *   *

It was dark in the barn. The only light was from a kerosene lantern on a bench casting its yellow glow across the floor and giving an eerie, shadowy appearance to the faces gathered. It had already been decided to hang the FEMA guy. After Emma Winston's suicide, the decision was immediate.

Brian and Rahn gathered a few soldiers. Linda and Donna insisted on being there, and I brought Craig with me. All in all, there were nine of us, not counting the condemned.

Rahn had made a noose, complete with 13 loops. He explained that the U.S. Army Regulation, 190-55 U.S. Army Corrections Systems: Procedures for Military Executions gave him a good idea on how to properly conduct and carry out an execution.

"Are you considering this guy military, then?" I asked.

"Not really, but I needed some kind of reference to make this official. I don't like the law of unintended consequences, and if we just hang him, it starts to look like a lynch mob. We don't want that type of justice for the future," he explained. "We even wrote up an execution order noting that he had been found guilty of rape, murder, and domestic terrorism activities. Brian signed it, and that's how we will explain it if and when anything is ever asked."

I nodded my understanding. "What will you do with the body?"

"I'm tempted to radio Wolfe and tell him to come and get it, but why poke the badger as an old friend of mine once said. We know he won't do it, and the less he knows about this the safer any of our people might be if they are ever captured."

"Good point," I said.

Rahn threw the rope over a crossbeam in the barn and tied one end to a support post. He then took a six-foot step ladder and placed it under the beam and looping the rope, rested the loop on top of the beam. He stepped down from the ladder.

"Bring him in," he said to two of the soldiers.

Two men, Klotz and Travis, went to the nearby horse stall and removed Minster. His hands were tied behind his back. Because he refused to walk, they each grabbed an arm, their hands tight around his upper biceps as they carried him by lifting him off of the ground, his bare feet dragging across the barn floor. They had dressed him earlier in his pants and shirt. There was no need for him to have boots and his were added to our supply of replacement equipment.

Klotz and Travis stopped in front of the ladder. Minster was shaking, tears flowed down his face. "C'mon, guys," he pleaded. "You don't want to do this."

Brian stepped in front of the group and looked at each of them. Clearing his throat a couple of times, he said, "Corey Minster, you have been found guilty of rape, murder, and domestic terrorism by a military court. You are hereby sentenced to be hung by the neck for these crimes until you are dead. Do you have any last words?"

"You can't do this. This is wrong. I was ordered to do it," he cried. Sobs began to rack his body and his knees gave out, causing him to slump to the floor.

Klotz and Travis pulled him back to his feet. Klotz remarked, "That excuse didn't work for the Nazis, either."

"At ease," Rahn said softly.

Klotz tightened his grip on Minster's arm.

"First Sergeant," Brian ordered.

They had rehearsed these steps earlier. Rahn moved forward with a pillowcase in his hand and placed it over Minster's head. Nodding at Klotz and Travis, the two men forced Minster up the ladder.

Awkwardly, Travis placed the noose around Minster's neck and tightened it. At the last minute, he remembered to place the knot behind his ear, the wrappings of it resting loosely across Minster's shoulders.

Keeping their hands on him, the two men stepped down off of the ladder.

Moving quickly, Rahn stepped forward and kicked the ladder away, causing Minster to drop, the rope going tight and instantly snapping his neck.

It was done.

The small group stood there, watching the body slowly swing and twist at the end of the rope.

"Is he dead?" Brian asked.

Rahn glanced at him, his eyebrows rising in a questioning manner. "We should wait a bit to make sure. A good 10 minutes should do it."

The group remained, silently watching as the slow swinging and twisting of the rope ended and the body hung there, motionless.

After a long silence, Travis spoke up. "What should we do with the body, Chief?"

"I'm tempted to feed it to the pigs," Brian said. "They can make it gone in no time, but we'll bury him. Klotz, Hart, and Bennet grab some shovels and go dig a hole. Four feet should be enough."

"Yes, sir," the men muttered.

*   *   *

After Emma's funeral, I checked in with Jake. We had spoken the evening before, and he had assembled his men into four teams. They were outfitted with the BaoFengs, their weapons, and several days' worth of rations—some MREs and some easy-to-keep meals that Nancy had created. Her skills were amazing.

"Everything ready, Jake?" I asked.

"They know what to do, John," he replied.

Still hanging onto the old standard of trust but verify, I went to the men as they tied their supplies to their horses. "You men understand you are to stay concealed and watch for these guys coming down the road. We don't know where they are going, so I want two men at Four Corners, two more near the turnoff where you leave 64 and head to White Lake, and two more on P where it turns east heading our way. The last two should be where you turn to head to Lake View. Any questions?"

"We understand, Mr. Henry," two of them said as the others nodded in agreement.

I decided not to tell them my name was John. It wasn't the time. "If you see anything, radio it in and tell us where they are going. Give us as much information about them as you can. Once we figure out where they are, haul ass back here."

With determined looks, the eight men mounted their horses. Four headed toward the front toward the bunker and the rest headed out across the meadow behind the cabin. They would ride cross country and take a more direct route.

The other two groups would watch from the two positions on County Highway P. The two men that would be at the White Lake turnoff more than likely would have several days of boredom, as I didn't really expect Wolfe and his men to go that far. My best guess was the other three teams would tell us what we needed to know.

Watching them ride off, Jake stepped toward me and asked, "Once we find them, what's next?"

"Good question. I don't know yet," I answered.

"I think we should attack," he offered.

"We might do that, Jake. We just might," I replied as I placed my hand on his shoulder, patting it.

I turned and headed back to the cabin. It was dinner time, and while I wasn't all that hungry,

I knew I had to eat. The next few days would be really active and food was fuel. I'd need that fuel because I wasn't planning on sitting on the porch for this one.

*   *   *

Wolfe was so excited he was almost shaking. The fuel bladder had arrived, and with a great deal of effort, he had Thomas and the men muscle it onto the bed of the 5-ton humvee. It was on there awkwardly but was durable enough to stay intact.

The team he and Thomas had picked, eight men plus an addition, one of the radio operators, were loading gear into the back of the 5-ton as well as the four HMMWVs. The day was warm but not hot. Wolfe had allowed the men to work in t-shirts, their black shade now darker from perspiration.

Stopping and putting his hands behind his back, Wolfe shouted, "Sergeant Thomas, a word."

Jogging away from the working men, Thomas went to Wolfe. "Yes, sir. What can I do for you?"

"That's unusually formal, isn't it, Thomas," Wolfe replied with a smirk.

"Sorry, sir. It's just that I'm a little tired from the loading and everything. I was trying to be polite."

Wolfe waved his hand dismissively. "I'm making a last-minute change."

"The radio operator, sir?" Thomas replied.

"No. I want you to keep three men rested. Carry out your training to classroom type instruction and stand by the radio in case we need backup. You have two Hummers and I want a QRF ready just in case. Eight men in two vehicles. Keep some ammo and MREs in them as well."

"So no physical training, Major?" Thomas asked, disappointment in his voice.

"No, nothing like that. I'm not in the habit of explaining my decisions, but I will this time. I'm trained in Infantry operations and that is basically what this is. You are better suited to training and disciplining these men. I want you to train them on working together and make them a team. I can't have you practicing patrolling around here because I need you ready in case I need you."

"Yes, sir," Thomas replied.

"You'll get your chance. When we rotate the teams, the people you have here will be yours out there. Then, there is phase two."

"If I may, what's phase two?"

"It should be obvious, Sergeant Thomas," Wolfe replied. "Phase two is when we all join together and destroy Henry, Rahn, and those other traitors."

*   *   *

Entering the kitchen, I smelled onions and something else. I wasn't sure what. The onions cooking on the stovetop were making my mouth water. I saw Nancy sitting at the table, which surprised me. She had taken over the role of head cook and no one questioned it. She had a notebook out and was writing in it.

Glancing toward the stove, I saw Donna and Linda working together with two large sizzling skillets.

Before I could say a word, Nancy said, "Fil, you aren't getting any until it's ready and everybody eats."

There was still a slight slurring of her words due to her wound, but this batch came out quick and clear, making me grin.

"I'm not joking, Fil. You'll wait like everyone else," she added.

"I wasn't laughing at you," I said. I was being watched and noticed out of my peripheral vision that Donna and Linda were glaring at me. The looks were not kind, and like the brave man I am, I chose to ignore them. "I'm hungry. When will dinner be ready?"

"Not for a couple of hours," Nancy replied.

That did not help me one bit, and as if to emphasize my current state, my stomach grumbled loudly.

"There's jerky in the cabinet behind you," Nancy said. "Grab a couple of pieces to tide you over, then get out of my kitchen."

"Yes, ma'am," I said, doing as she instructed and going back out the way I came.

I decided to walk over to the gardens, chewing on the jerky as I went. An abundance of produce was there with green tomatoes, beans, squash, cucumbers, and zucchini growing everywhere. In fact, the entire garden, many times the size I'd had that we started with, was doing very well.

While I was contemplating how much we could harvest and remembering what we had to do to get seeds from this batch for next year's crop, I heard footsteps padding in the dirt behind me. Looking over my shoulder, I could see it was Linda.

I turned back and continued staring at the garden. After our last conversation, I wasn't sure she had anything to say that I wanted to hear. Following this morning's funeral and last night's event, I didn't think I had anything more to say, either. So, I kept silent, for all of about 10 seconds.

"Hello, Linda."

"John," she said, "I'm still upset."

I didn't reply. I just stood there, chewing on my jerky and watching the plants grow. I did not want to have this conversation.

"But I get it."

"Do you?" I asked, hoping the skepticism I felt wasn't betrayed by my tone.

"I do. Emma didn't ask for any of this. Those people came, killed her family, did that to her sister-in-law, and for what? For what, John?"

"I don't have an answer for you. There is evil in this world and it is alive and well right here in Wisconsin."

"There has to be some place without evil. Someplace where people are decent. Not perfect, just decent. I know what it's like to lose family. I can only begin to imagine what Emma was feeling."

"I don't know what you want me to say," I offered.

"Just stand there and listen. Sometimes, you men... Men can't fix everything. You can't fix this. I don't know what can."

"We just have to stick together, Linda. It's what friends and family do. We are all one big family, a family of friends."

"I don't know about that," Linda said. "It seems to me that people who you make friends with seem to die." She put her hand to her mouth and quickly apologized. "Oh my God, John. I didn't mean that. I'm sorry."

"Don't worry about it," I replied, extending my arms toward her for an embrace.

She shook her head, her eyes starting to water. "No, I can't. I'm sorry." She turned back to go to the cabin.

"Damn," I uttered, watching her as she marched toward the back door. "Damn."

CHAPTER 15

"Because night has fallen and the barbarians haven't come."

—C.P. Cavafy

Wolfe stood next to the lead vehicle in the five-vehicle convoy. There were two more behind him, then the 5-ton and a HMMWV trailing.

Edmiston had taken on the role of driver for Wolfe and was enjoying his newfound stature amongst the other men. Wolfe looked down the line and then turned, making eye contact with Thomas, who was standing just outside the armory door. He gave Thomas a nod, stuck his arm in the air, his index finger pointing skyward and moved his arm in a circular motion, signaling the men to start their engines. The vehicles came to life as their drivers started them up.

Wolfe climbed into the lead HMMWV and said, "Move out, Edmiston," and the convoy began its journey.

Edmiston drove forward and turned right out of the armory, heading toward Highway 45. After a short drive, he took a left turn onto Highway 64 going east. It wasn't long before the town of Antigo was behind them, and the scattered farmhouses, seemingly abandoned, began to appear along the road.

"Keep us at no more than 45 miles an hour, Edmiston. I don't want that fuel bladder damaged," Wolfe ordered.

"Yes, sir." Edmiston looked at the speedometer and settled in for the drive.

It wasn't long before they approached the town of Polar. Edmiston noticed a bar and grill on their left and glanced at Wolfe. "Hey, Major, there's a place we could stop for a beer and food, if you're hungry."

Wolfe gave Edmiston a look that told him his humor was not welcome.

The small convoy continued along 64, seeing no other signs of vehicles or people. Wisps of smoke from some of the houses off the road signaled that some people were still out there, but Wolfe didn't see anyone.

"Do you know where to turn?" Wolfe asked.

"County Highway P," Edmiston answered. "Should be about another 15 minutes or so."

"When you make the turn, slow down and allow the others to tighten up on us. The map says there is a church there, so pull into the church parking lot."

"Yes, sir."

The convoy continued until County P, where, as instructed, Edmiston turned right, and then a quick right took him into the church parking lot. Wolfe ordered him to pull forward into a larger blacktopped area and stop.

Exiting the vehicle, Wolfe watched as the other vehicles stopped in line. He made a striking motion across his throat, signaling the men to turn off their vehicles.

Using both arms, he made a pulling motion to signal everyone to come to him.

All of the men left their vehicles and walked toward the major.

"Smoke 'em if you got 'em," Wolfe said.

Some of the men took cigarettes out of their pockets and did as instructed. The remainder stood there, waiting to hear what was next.

"Alright, men, listen up. We are not far from where we will set up for our operation. From this point forward, I want everyone to keep their eyes open and watch for any sign of the people who left us and joined up with Henry and his band. When we get to our base area, tents need to be set up first and be careful of that fuel bladder. All weapons, if not already, should be locked and loaded. Any questions?"

"Major, what are our rules of engagement?" one man asked.

"For today and tonight, we will shoot only if fired on. We'll discuss the rules when we send out patrols tomorrow. Any other questions?" Wolfe let his eyes travel to each of the men in front of him. When he decided there were no further questions, he ordered them back into their vehicles and gave the signal to move out.

Edmiston drove in a circle and left the parking lot the same way he had entered, then turned left to go south on County P toward the hatchery.

*   *   *

Two pairs of eyes watched the FEMA convoy from across the road. One of the men, once he was certain of the direction they were going, picked up his BaoFeng dual-band radio and made a call.

"Base, Base, this is team one. We have contact heading south. Four Hummers, a truck. Looks like 12 people and a lot of equipment, over."

"Team one, this is Base. Roger, out."

"Base, this is team two, we are ready, over." The call came from the second of the teams on County P, located about two miles west of the hatchery, near a crossroads.

"Teams three and four, this is Base. Return home, over."

*   *   *

I saw Rahn and Brian heading my way, so I waited for them. No sense my walking to meet them, too, part of being older and wiser. As they approached, I couldn't help myself. "Well, if it isn't Mutt and Jeff," I said.

"Who?" they both replied.

Obviously, they weren't as cultured as I was and missed the old Sunday Comics reference. It was better than accepting that they thought I was old.

"So what brings you two out here?" I asked.

"Wolfe is in the neighborhood," Rahn answered. "They're on County P and heading this way."

"What are they coming with?"

"Four Hummers, a truck, about 12 men, plus equipment. It's obvious they're going to set up somewhere. The second team on P is waiting. We'll know more when they get eyes on them."

I looked at Brian. "So, what's the plan? You going to hit them before they get set up?"

"That and more," Brian said.

"More? What's more?" I asked, surprised.

A flurry of activity toward the barn distracted me as I saw several soldiers putting equipment in vehicles and loading weapons.

"We're going to hit them hard as soon as we know where they're stopping. Just a quick raid to let them know we know they're here," Brian explained.

"That isn't the *more*," I said. "What's the more?"

"We're planning to hit the armory, too," Rahn said.

"You're going to split our forces and hit two targets?" I asked. The tone of my voice betrayed my feelings. "I thought splitting a force was a serious do-not-do-that move."

"If they have 12 here, then they only have 12 to 18 there. We have a superior force, plus they don't know that we know what they're doing."

"When will you hit the first group?"

"I'm guessing within the next hour or two. I'm sending three teams with SAWs for a quick raid. Once we know where they are, we'll rush in, shoot shit up and rush out," Brian said. "The teams will go on to Lake View shortly and wait. Once we know, we'll do a hasty plan and execute it."

"Won't they radio back and tell the armory they were hit?" I asked.

"Won't matter. The people at the armory can't do anything about it. Besides, it should come as no surprise to them that we'll do something. Wolfe is an egomaniac, but even he should know they can't expect to not be challenged," Rahn replied. "We won't stay on target longer than a quick drive through, maybe disable some of their Hummers and take out some of their force."

"And if we get casualties?"

"John, you can't expect to fight a war and not have casualties," Rahn answered. "You know that."

I shrugged. I did know. "Who's leading the first assault?"

"I am," Brian said. "Rahn will lead the assault on the armory. He knows it better than I do."

I turned to look at Rahn. "Who's going on that assault?"

"I thought I'd take Johnson, Roop, and a couple of Jake's guys. If we don't include them, they'll feel left out or taken advantage of. We can't do that," Rahn explained. "I thought I'd take Craig and Hart, too."

"Craig's not trained for this," I quickly said.

"Dad, Craig has more than shown he knows what he's doing. We have to take him. He's already been there once."

I pursed my lips together. "I don't like it."

"You can't hide him from the world forever, Dad," Brian said. "He should go."

"Then, you can tell his mother. I'll go with you, but you get to tell Donna. They'll need to be ready in case we have casualties anyway."

"Let's go then."

"Nancy won't be happy, either."

"I'm a soldier, and she's a soldier's wife. She'll handle it okay," Brian said.

Heading toward the cabin, he looked back at me over his shoulder and said, "Let's go." His grin gave me the courage I needed to face what I knew would be three unhappy women.

"I'll do the final equipment check and briefing," Rahn said as he swiftly went toward the barn and the assembling soldiers there.

"Coward," Brian shouted.

"You betchya," was Rahn's reply.

Rahn didn't take five steps before Sajan came running up to him, handing him a piece of paper. The two exchanged a few words before Rahn trotted back to where Brian and I were standing.

"We've got them," he announced enthusiastically.

"Where?" I replied.

"They're at the fish hatchery. I'm sending the team out now. Jake's people will meet the team just before the entrance to the hatchery; give them the latest information and then let us work our magic."

"Good luck," was all I could think to say.

Brian left me standing near the porch. He ran back toward the three HMMWVs and hopped into the lead vehicle. They sped off out of the barnyard and out our front road. The battle was on, and now I did have to tell Donna to get ready.

*   *   *

The small convoy pulled onto the road to the fish hatchery as if they already owned the place, which in a manner of speaking, they did. There were a few white frame government buildings and a lot of trash thrown about on the ground. Edmiston, at Wolfe's direction, drove the vehicles around in a circle, orienting them to face back toward the entrance road.

Stepping out of the lead vehicle, Wolfe put his hands on his hips and began to visually survey the area. "Edmiston," he shouted.

"Yes, Major?"

"Go check out that smaller building; see if it's suitable for a headquarters."

"Yes, sir," Edmiston said and headed toward a small building raised on concrete block piers. He walked up the three steps, and standing on the small porch, opened the front door.

The smell almost made him gag. Piles of trash was strewn around the room. Putting his hand over his mouth and nose, he began to look around. There was a front room, open to the door, and behind it, another two rooms. Inspecting these, he saw one was an office that had sleeping bags and a mattress. The other was the bathroom, the origins of the odors. Human waste was all over the room, and it appeared that either the toilet was broken or there was no water for the toilet.

Edmiston made a hasty retreat out of the building. Stopping for a minute to catch his breath and clear his lungs, he began to move again, heading toward Wolfe.

"Major," he said as he came upon the tall, curly brown-haired leader of the group.

"Yes," Wolfe answered.

"I think you could use it for a headquarters. There's trash and stuff in there, and the bathroom is in serious need of a cleaning."

"How bad is the bathroom?" Wolfe asked. "It'd be nice not to have to use a slit trench latrine."

"It's pretty bad, Major."

"Get somebody on it, and let's get these tents set up on either side of the building. When you get that bathroom cleaned out and the trash removed, I'll move in there," Wolfe ordered as he used his thumb to point at the building.

*   *   *

Brian, along with his three HMMWV assault force, stopped on County Highway P as two of Jake's scouts came out of the tree line about a quarter of a mile from the entrance to the armory. Not worrying about other vehicle traffic, they simply halted in the middle of the road, the SAW gunners in each of the three vehicles automatically scanning the area in front and behind them.

Brian got out of his vehicle and leaving the door open, proceeded to walk toward the two scouts, meeting them about halfway from where they came out of the woods.

"What do you have for me?" he asked.

One of the scouts, Dave, said, "There are four HMMWVs and a big army truck loaded up with equipment. It drove into the hatchery. I know there are several buildings in there and a circular driveway about a thousand yards inside. The area is wide open with just a couple of pines standing."

"How many men?" Brian asked. "We've been told about a dozen."

"That's about right," Dave confirmed.

"Any sign of automatic weapons?"

"You mean like machine guns?" Dave asked, raising his eyebrows.

Grinning, Brian realized these men were not soldiers. "Yeah, like machine guns."

"I didn't see anything like you guys have," Dave replied, using his chin to point toward the mounted SAWs on the three HMMWVs.

"Excellent," Brian said. "You guys go back inside the trees. We're going to attack and then run like hell out of there. We need you to stay here, let us know if they come after us, and then make sure they don't get reinforcements. I'll let Jake know when we get back and get you guys relieved."

"Sounds good, Sarge," Dave said.

"I'm a chief," Brian said automatically. "We'll head in there in about five minutes."

"Okay, Chief," Dave said. He walked back to the other scout, where the two scouts spoke briefly. Then, they went inside the tree line and Brian quickly lost sight of them.

He went to the two trailing vehicles and explained the layout. He reminded each of the teams what the plan was. Returning to his vehicle, he closed the door and said, "Okay, Specialist Johnson, let's go. One quick run in and out."

"Roger," Johnson replied and accelerated down the road toward the hatchery entrance.

Once he made the turn, Johnson waited a second for the other two vehicles to catch up, then he pushed the gas pedal down as hard as he could. The three HMMWVs lurched forward rapidly, picking up speed.

Brians's gunner, PFC Owens, saw the lined-up vehicles in front of him. Leaning into the butt of the SAW, he waited for Brian's order to fire. He didn't have to wait long.

"NOW Owens!" Brian shouted.

Owens began firing controlled bursts until they were alongside the four black HMMWVs.

The three HMMWVs raced along the side of the FEMA vehicles firing indiscriminately into the black objects as they passed each one.

Men jumped out of vehicles. Some were falling over as they tried to run, while a few remained in the vehicles, the shocked looks on their faces demonstrating the surprise Brian wanted to achieve.

As they drove forward, Brian saw Major Wolfe. Tempted to wave at him as they raced by, he decided not to, the rapid-fire of the SAWs sending a clear message. *I hope somebody shoots that son of a bitch.*

Johnson drove to the end of the line of FEMA vehicles and made a loop to drive back out of the hatchery while allowing the gunners to continue to shoot into the vehicles.

It was clear Johnson almost forgot to slow down on the drive out of the hatchery and had to hit the brakes hard to make the turn.

*   *   *

The sudden roar of engines stopped Wolfe's conversation as first one, then another, and then a third military HMMWV raced into the area shooting at them with mounted Squad Automatic Weapons. Dropping to the ground and crawling on his stomach under the black HMMWV he had arrived in, Wolfe stared at the three vehicles firing indiscriminately on them.

Henry.

The lead vehicle raced by him, and he saw a man sitting in the passenger side of the lead HMMWV. Wolfe reached for the drop holster and grabbed the grip of his M9, 9mm sidearm, and began shooting at the vehicles as they raced around the compound. He had emptied his magazine before he realized he was the only one shooting back at the three vehicles.

Reloading with some difficulty as he lay under the vehicle, he was able to chamber a round just as the trailing HMMWV raced by him and headed down the entrance road. In an act of defiance, Wolfe pointed his weapon at the trailing vehicle and emptied his 15-round magazine toward it, screaming obscenities as he did so.

"I'll fucking kill you, Henry," he shouted as the slide locked back on his weapon, signaling he had fired his last round.

"Edmiston," Wolfe shouted.

"Yes sir," came a voice nearby from under the HMMWV.

"Get your ass out here," Wolfe ordered.

Edmiston crawled out from under the vehicle and slowly stood, dusting himself off of the dirt, grass, and other debris he had managed to pick up under the vehicle during the attack. "Yes sir," Edmiston said again as he continued to wipe his hands across his uniform.

"Get me a casualty count and a damage assessment," Wolfe ordered. As he told Edmiston what to do, he visually inspected what he could see from where he was.

The fuel bladder was leaking fuel badly and the 5-ton it was on had more holes than swiss cheese. *Fuck.* He reached inside of his vehicle for the radio handset. Pushing the talk button, he said, "Antigo Base, this is Antigo 6, over."

"Antigo 6, this is Base over."

"Antigo Base, get me Antigo 8 ASAP, over."

"Antigo 6, stand by."

Wolfe held the microphone at his side as he surveyed the destruction of his team. The 5-ton was destroyed and all of the HMMWVs had damage. He saw several of his men lying on the ground in awkward positions suggesting they were dead. Edmiston was speaking with several men who were either giving first aid to the wounded or apparently not sure about what they should be doing.

"Antigo 6, this is Antigo 8, over," Platoon Sergeant Thomas said as he came on the line.

"This is Antigo 6. We've been attacked, over. Request immediate assistance."

*   *   *

Safely making the right turn back onto County Highway P, the three team convoy raced back to the cabin to begin preparations for the next phase of their assault on FEMA.

As they drove by the Qwik Mart, Brian shouted, "Stop!" causing Johnson to slam on the brakes.

Hopping out of the stopped HMMWV, he ran back to the trailing HMMWV and opened the driver's door. "Specialist Klause, I want you to conceal your vehicle in that rubble and remain here in case they follow us. Do *not* let them pass." He'd recognized it as the same collection of debris that Hart and Roop had once used when they surprised the FEMA patrol and gained an extra vehicle as their prize.

"Roger, Chief," Klause said.

"I'll send someone to either relieve your team or we'll radio you to come in," Brian instructed.

Klause nodded and turned his vehicle toward the rubble.

Brian went back to his vehicle, climbed in, and said, "Let's go home, Johnson."

"Roger that, Chief."

CHAPTER 16

"The angel of death has been abroad
throughout the land; You may almost hear
the beating of his wings."

—John Bright

Platoon Sergeant Thomas was conflicted. After Wolfe had explained the attack and casualties—four dead, three wounded, the 5-ton inoperable, and the fuel bladder leaking like a sieve—he began to experience doubt. *These guys are better than the major thought they were. We aren't trained for this. I don't know what he expects us to do, but we can't continue this hunt he seems to be on. We've lost too much. We can't leave people here, either.*

The instructions had been clear. Thomas was to send another HMMWV with four men to reinforce Wolfe. He was to radio Wausau and ask for additional resources, explaining that Wolfe had engaged with the people he was after and needed more support.

Standing up from the chair he occupied in the communications room, Thomas took a deep breath. What poor four unfortunates do I send out to Wolfe?

*   *   *

Rahn and I were waiting for Brian when he came back home to our growing assembly of people and equipment. He had radioed ahead that the mission was a complete success and that they had no casualties. Brian was pleased, and when the look on his face almost instantly relaxed at the news, I knew he was feeling the stress of our situation more than I thought.

Brian exited his vehicle and said something to Johnson and the other driver. He then joined us.

"I left Klause and Travis at the Qwik Mart as rear security. We hurt them bad, but I don't want any surprises," he explained after we had shook hands and congratulated him on his success.

"How long are you going to leave them there?" Rahn asked.

"I figure till dark. After that, we can bring them in. Jake's boys are still scouting and I need to see what Jake wants to do with them," Brian said. "We left the other team out there as an advance warning."

Rahn said, "I pulled the team from White Lake. We know where they are going now."

Brian asked, "You ready to brief the Antigo party-goers?"

"Yeah, we need to get that underway. How are we on fuel?" Rahn asked.

"There's still diesel at the Qwik Mart and we should go get some soon. We have all of the vehicles except your three fully fueled."

"Oh, all one of them," Rahn said sarcastically.

"Time to catch up, First Sergeant. We got the FEMA Hummer working now," Brian said.

"Well, I'll be damned," Rahn replied.

"I'm still concerned about this armory raid," I interjected, tired of being ignored. "How many men are you taking, and how undefended will we be here with you taking three vehicles and the SAWs?"

"We're only taking one SAW," Brian explained, "and it will be dismounted. We're also taking four National Guard men, a couple of Jake's guys, one of which will be Jake because he's insisting, Craig, Sajan, and Donna."

"Donna," I said, surprised. "You're taking Donna?"

"Yeah, she and I talked about it before we came to see you. We figured we'd need a medic if somebody was hurt on the raid. If we have her, then she can take care of them, get them stable, and then we can transport here. We'll take the FEMA Hummer and one other. Before you ask, it's the royal *we*. I'm not going; this is Rahn's mission."

"I still don't like the idea of Craig going, and who decided on Sajan," I said.

"He asked if he could go. He has a good head on his shoulders, Dad. We need to get these people more combat experience, and this shouldn't be that hard of a mission. It's mostly sneaking, shooting shit up, and leaving."

"For the record, I don't like it, but it's your call," I said with a bit too much resignation.

"Craig wants to talk to you," Brian added. "He said it's important."

"Where is he?" I asked.

"Where is he always," Brian said jovially.

As I walked toward the cabins to hear what Craig wanted, I saw Allen bring something to Rahn and Brian. He had been spending time with

Sam again and I was certain it was some kind of message. I'd find out later.

I stepped up onto the porch of the cabin where Addie lived. Her door was open. It was still a bit warm, and I'm sure she wanted the breeze. I stood in front of her door. Addie and Craig were sitting inside on a couch we had taken from Quint's place.

I knocked on the door jamb, but before I could say anything, Craig said, "Come on in, Dad."

Stepping inside, I took an old dining room chair they had and sat on it, the back of the chair in front of my chest. "Brian said you wanted to see me," I said.

"Yes," he answered. "We have something to tell you."

As soon as he said it a chill ran through my body. That quick flashing chill that I hoped did not make me shudder.

"What do you want to tell me?" I asked, trying hard not to show any emotion other than simple curiosity.

"Um, uh, we…" Craig began.

"Oh, Craig," Addie interrupted. "John, you're going to be a grandfather."

"And Addie and I are getting married, Dad." Craig grinned as he squeezed Addie's hand.

I was glad I was sitting down.

*　　*　　*

To say that Major Elias Wolfe was angry would have been a monumental understatement of epic proportions. He had four dead men, three wounded men. His fuel bladder had emptied onto the ground, having been shot full of holes, and his five remaining men were grumbling and glaring at him as he made them cannibalize two of the HMMWVs to get at least one working.

He sent one of the men out to the entrance to keep watch. The man paced back and forth across the road.

Edmiston had spent most of the time after the attack cleaning out the building Wolfe intended to use as his headquarters. It was also now a place for the others to stay as well.

Those other guys can clean out this bathroom. I ain't doing it. The pungent obnoxious odor of human waste still poured out of the room. He had managed to open some of the windows, breaking one because it had been painted shut. The heavy sound of boots on the wood floor announced that someone had come inside.

Turning around quickly, he saw the major, a look of disgust on his face as the odor of garbage and human waste assaulted him. "Edmiston, get that bathroom cleaned out," Wolfe ordered.

"Yes, sir," Edmiston mumbled.

"What was that?" Wolfe asked sharply.

"I said, yes sir."

"Well, get on it then. We can't sleep in here with that stink. Get one of the other men to help you. We have more people coming, and I want this ready."

Seeing his chance to avoid some unpleasantness, Edmiston rushed out of the building and ran to where the other men were. "One of you guys come here," he shouted.

One of the younger guys, not experienced enough to have learned you never look at someone shouting made that mistake and Edmiston had his man.

"Come on now, hurry. The major has another job for you."

Picking up his M4, the man did as he was instructed.

He'll probably want to shoot me with that when he sees what I have for him. Tough shit.

*　　　*　　　*

I was in a bit of shock. My youngest son was going to be a father. AND…he said he and Addie were going to get married. I was worried and excited, proud and scared all at the same time. We had sat and talked for quite a while there in the cabin.

Addie was a woman and not the same person who had joined us a few short months ago. I'd seen Craig change and grow a lot in that time, too. From our first encounter back in Appleton when we defended Donna's house to the fight with the looters to his sniper action with the bikers and then more recently, Rahn's scouting trip to the armory. Craig was no longer my baby, and even though I'd always look at him that way, his and my burden to bear, him growing up was not something I was prepared for. My God, we had to have a wedding in the middle of our war for survival. We had a wedding and a baby to plan for… I needed a drink.

I went into the cabin through the back door and to the kitchen. Donna and Nancy were sitting at the table, talking and laughing. That was good to see. It was as if nothing had changed and all that we had experienced was a bad dream. I said hello as I walked by.

Nancy said, "Craig is looking for you, Fil."

I mumbled thanks and kept on walking. Going into my room, I got a cigar from my hiding place, grabbed a bottle of whiskey, poured a glass, and went out onto the porch.

Sitting in my chair, I went through the ritual of cutting and lighting my cigar. Max and King came over and curled up alongside my chair. *Odd. They must know I've got a lot on my mind.*

I sat there for a while as darkness took over, sipping my whiskey and enjoying my cigar. This is how I liked to think things through. I didn't get a chance to do this often. Someone always managed to show up and want to talk.

That must have been a premonition. The screen door squeaked open, announcing someone coming outside.

It was Linda.

She came over and sat in the chair next to me. "Penny for your thoughts," she said.

"That's an old expression," I said. "I didn't expect to hear something like that from you."

"We live in Wisconsin, John. We do and say a lot of old things."

"I guess you're right." Then, I saw it. She raised a glass to her lips and sipped.

"Is that my whiskey?" I asked in a not unfriendly tone.

"Maybe," she teased. "I went to your room to look for you and saw it sitting on your dresser. So

I took a glass, knew where you were, and came out here. You did offer…if you recall."

I have to admit, it isn't always welcome when you know someone who doesn't forget things you say. Before I could object, she took another sip and said, "I want to talk to you."

"What about?"

"I wanted to apologize for the way I jumped at you about the FEMA guy."

I half-shrugged. "You don't need to do that."

"Yes, I do. I don't agree with torture and that won't change. But as my dad used to say, some men need killing and he was one that did."

"You always have this way of surprising me, Linda."

"What do you mean by that?" she asked.

"You've never striked me as the capital punishment kind of person. Not that I think you're against it. I just didn't picture you as someone who thought it was a good idea. Especially the way we did it."

"It was done right. Remember, I was there. I witnessed it. I was still upset about Emma. That was hard."

"I know," I said as I took a draw from my cigar, blew the smoke out, and took a long sip of whiskey. For some reason, I was nervous.

It was dark, and while I could see her in the shadows of the night, her features were hidden. I like to see people's faces when I talk with them, and I couldn't see hers. I felt a bit lost in the conversation.

Her hand found it's way onto my forearm where it rested on the arm of my chair. The roughness of her hand was still there and I realized I liked that roughness. Just like the time I took her hand out in the meadow.

"I'm not mad at you or at anyone here. Sometimes, it just gets the best of me. So much going on, and I react."

All I could think to do was take another sip of my drink as we sat silently for a moment.

Breaking that silence, she said, "This is where you are supposed to say something."

Thinking quickly, I said, "It's okay to react like that. We all do at some point. It's part of being human, and it shows that you have human feelings."

"Thank you," she replied. "You're good to talk to."

"I try to be a good listener, although Brian and Craig may sometimes disagree with that."

Linda laughed. "I know Donna sometimes does."

"Oh, what did she say?"

"We're all kind of on top of each other here. We all have our moments."

One thing I had learned about Linda was that she could be evasive and ambiguous at times. I think it's a female thing, though. Changing the subject, I asked, "How's the whiskey?"

"It's good. Thank you for sharing it."

I smirked. "I didn't exactly share it."

"You did offer; I remember that."

"Yes, I did."

Her hand was still on my arm and its warmth was creeping slowly up and down my arm. I kept my arm still. I was beginning to like it. That made me feel guilty. Carol hadn't been gone all that long and here I was enjoying the touch, innocent as it may be, of another woman.

"Would you like a cigar, too?"

"I detect sarcasm," she replied.

"Kind of. But if you want one—"

"I quit a long time ago. I think the last time I had one I took one of my brother's. I ended up getting sick afterwards."

"I didn't know you had a brother."

She nodded. "He's in the air force in Illinois."

"Oh, I didn't know," I replied, repeating myself.

"What's going to happen next?" she asked. There was that ambiguity again. Was she speaking about her hand on my arm or was she talking about something else?

"What do you mean?" I asked, taking the safer approach.

"I know they're planning to attack the armory, and the FEMA guys aren't that far away. I'm worried, John. I have two little boys; I need to be concerned with their safety."

"Rahn and Brian are taking care of that. They hurt the FEMA guys pretty bad, and after they hit the armory maybe they'll leave us alone."

"Do you really believe that?"

"I have to. I can't think of anything else." I took another draw of my cigar before a sip of the whiskey. "It's in my nature to be as positive as I can." *That's bull shit, and you know it, John Henry. You're as worried as everyone else is.*

The clearing of a throat just off the porch startled us both. "Brian, is that you," I said.

"Sorry to interrupt, but we need to talk," he answered, not coming up on the porch.

"I should leave you two." Linda stood, pressing her hand into my arm as she did so. She moved her hand away, and as she left she brushed it gently across the back of my head and went inside.

As she entered the cabin, Brian came up on the porch and sat down in the now vacant chair next to me.

"Bad timing," he said.

I could sense his smirk in the dark. "As always," I replied. "So, what do we need to talk about?"

"Another Hummer just entered the hatchery."

*   *   *

Edmiston waved the arriving HMMWV into the drive. The wide vehicle navigated the turn a little sharply, causing him to have to jump out of the way. Wolfe could hear the laughter coming from inside the vehicle that told him it wasn't accidental.

As the HMMWV edged toward the building that was now the headquarters, Wolfe stood waiting for it on the step. With his hands clasped behind his back, he rocked back and forth on his heels, his impatience showing.

When the four men exited the vehicle, he let his frustration over the day rise up. "What took you so long," he demanded.

"We weren't exactly sure where to go, Major," the driver replied. "We also didn't want to get ambushed on the way here, so we were extra cautious."

Ignoring what he saw as an excuse, Wolfe asked, "So it's just the four of you? What else did Sergeant Thomas send?"

"Major, we have two cases of 5.56 ammo and a case of MREs. When we left, Sergeant Thomas told us he was still trying to get Wausau to send us more supplies. He gave me this letter for you," the driver said as he handed an envelope to Wolfe.

"You men unload your vehicle and find a place to lay down your gear inside. Our tents were shot up, and for now, this is the best we can do. We'll look at one of the other buildings tomorrow." Without waiting for a response, Wolfe walked indoors and went straight to his room and office, which consisted of a folding field table, a multi-fuel green camping lantern, and a folding metal chair. A GI issue cot had been set up against the wall with an unrolled sleeping bag on top of it.

Glancing around his room for any unwelcome eyes watching him, Wolfe walked to the table. Sitting on the chair, he opened the envelope.

Sir,

I'm sorry to deliver this information to you this way, but after your being attacked I thought that maybe someone was listening in on your radio trans-

missions. I thought this was the best for Operational Security.

I have made several attempts to get the extra supplies from Wausau. The Supply people said I needed authorization from you, and after some creative discussion, we overcame that issue. However, the problem now is the Regional Administrator. Mr. Barstow isn't real keen on giving us more supplies. He said he just sent you some and wanted to know why that wasn't enough.

I explained to him about the attack and that some equipment was destroyed or seriously damaged. He asked me how that happened, and I explained that you were attacked by multiple mobile forces armed with automatic weapons. That did not make him very happy.

He said he would do what he could, but their supplies were low as well. He was sending out parties to procure food and other things needed to operate the camps and our region. He also said to tell you that he is contacting Madison to ask for more assistance. He was not sure if that would be National Guard or more FEMA people.

I told him we were fighting elements of the National Guard here and that maybe using more of them wasn't a good idea. He told me you had said the same thing. When the supplies get here, I will contact you and have one of our teams bring it to you. We are down to two HMMWVs here, Sir. I was wondering if maybe we should move from here and join you in the field?

Platoon Sergeant Thomas

Wausau Region FEMA

"I'll have to think about this," Wolfe said aloud. "Right now, I have other things to worry about."

*   *   *

Rahn assembled the National Guard soldiers in the barn, along with Craig, Sajan, and Rick. The men were all chatting amongst themselves as soldiers do when they don't know what's going on.

Even the three men who weren't soldiers were engaging in the idle speculation and bravado.

"Okay, men, listen up," Rahn announced. "When the chief gets here we will divide into two teams, one for the primary mission and the other for enhanced local security. He'll explain the plan and how we will execute it."

"I'm here, First Sergeant," Brian said as he joined the group. "I want the following men to form up over here to my right. Johnson, Roop, Hart, Henry, and Sajan. You are the primary mission team. The First Sergeant will give you your instructions. The rest of you fall in on me. You are the enhanced security team."

Rahn joined his team and began to explain the operation. "Okay, men, listen carefully. Jake and Donna will also be joining us. I'll brief Jake later, and Donna is going as medical support if we need it. We will move out through the woods and logging roads in two vehicles. Our departure time is false dawn."

"What's false dawn?" Sajan asked.

"Just before sunrise. It will look like the sun is rising, but it's just its glow below the horizon and not an actual sunrise. Our goal is to reach the assembly point we used when we scouted the armory. We'll hide in place till dark and then move, using the same route to the woods behind the armory. We will then wait till midnight and assault the armory. The first step will be silent sentry removal."

"Does that mean what I think it means?" Craig asked.

"Indeed it does, and you will be one of those men doing it. Knives only, gentlemen. You might want to get that knife back from your brother, Craig."

"I have it," Craig replied coldly.

Continuing, Rahn said, "Once we take out the sentries, we'll enter the armory, rush the assembly hall where most of them are sleeping and hit the communications room, which is close to my old office. We aren't staying there long. This is a hit and run mission. The purpose is to let them know we can reach out and touch them and that there's nothing they can do about it."

"We've got a lot of people here, First Sergeant. Do we need this many?" Specialist Hart asked.

"We believe there are now a dozen, possibly more, possibly less, at the armory. I want to be certain we have enough to do the assault, provide security for the assault force, and ensure we all get back. Craig and Jake will do the sentry removal. The preliminary plan now is for you, Roop, Sajan, and myself to do the assault. Jake and Craig will pull back and provide rear security while Johnson and Sajan will provide security at our CP behind the Containers business."

"Roger, First Sergeant," Hart replied.

"Assault team Hart, Roop, Sajan. Our assault will be swift and violent. Once we breach the building through the doors, we will aggressively move to the armory hall and communications room. Hart and Sajan will go to the hall, Roop and I will take the communications room. Shoot it up, share some frags, and get out. We will be inside for less than one minute."

"How many sentries?" a new voice asked.

Jake had just arrived and waited until Rahn was finished explaining the assault team's duties.

"Two, Jake. That's all we saw when we did our reconnaissance and that's all the FEMA guy told us they had. With at least half of their force being in our backyard, I doubt they'll double or increase security."

"And if they do, Jake, we can handle it," Craig added.

Jake turned and winked at Craig. The act was not lost on Rahn.

"As far as equipment, everyone gets an M-4. And carries five magazines. Each gets two frags. I want two bags, one in each Hummer, with five more magazines per team member and two frags each. We'll also take one of the SAWs and a box of belted ammo for it. Shouldn't need more than that."

"I don't have one of your fancy soldier weapons, Top," Jake said.

"I'll get you one," Rahn answered. "You know how to use it?"

"I was Cav, Top," Jake answered.

"Okay, do you know how to use it *without* hurting yourself?" Rahn's reply caused a chuckle to ripple through the group, easing the natural tension and nerves before a mission.

Jake raised his arm and saluted Rahn with an extended middle finger, causing the laughter to become even more pronounced.

"Any other questions," Rahn asked.

Silence greeted him.

"Alright then, you know what to do. Get ready, and be here at zero four-thirty. Jake, let's go get you that weapon."

"I'd like to bring a couple of my guys," Jake said. "They are feeling a bit left out, and they know how to handle themselves."

"Pick two of the former marines. We don't have time to check anyone out on tactics and they'll be able to step right in."

*   *   *

FEMA Regional Administrator Rick Barstow had received news that a replacement team of FEMA Guards under the command of Colonel Wayne Harrigan was due within the hour. As he played with the pencil-thin mustache on his lip, he imagined the surprise this force would bring to the remaining National Guard soldiers, whose loyalty he questioned, and the boost in morale for his small FEMA Guard contingent still remaining at the Wausau camps. The promised team, of over 50 men he had been told, would allow him to not only reinforce his existing teams but could give his advanced team in Antigo much needed manpower.

Formed in the early 2000s, the FEMA Guard had been a quasi-secretive force developed for situations just like this—to provide needed security and enforcement of protocols that ensured the new government to properly care for the new society created following a catastrophic event. The irony to all of it was how he had the National Guard members still in the Wausau camp setting up housing and other necessities to care for these new arrivals.

Rick knew they had no idea what would happen when they arrived. The headquarters in the former middle school across the road from the county fairgrounds was abuzz. Administrative personnel were scurrying around, moving office furniture and equipment so that the new arrivals had space to work and coordinate their activities. Placing two armed guards at the entrance, Barstow had given orders that only FEMA personnel could enter the building.

Through his window, he could see across the road where a team of soldiers was setting up tents so that some of the civilian residents could be moved out of the fairground buildings they were currently living in. Army Sergeant Bill Stillwater was leading the teams as they erected several general purpose large tents with liners and the diesel stoves that would heat them in colder weather. A medium height man with broad shoulders and a no-nonsense approach to work, Stillwater was pushing his men hard to complete the tasks they had been assigned.

"Hurry up," he shouted. "They want these tents up 15 minutes ago."

Silently, the soldiers continued their work as they pulled on ropes that stretched the heavy canvases and gave shape to the row of tents.

Another group was unrolling concertina wire in a perimeter around the tent area. The rows were established in a pyramid shape by stacking them on top of each other, effectively building a barrier that would discourage anyone from trying to go over or through them. An entranceway was created at each end, allowing people to enter or leave as needed.

"Who's going to be staying here, Sergeant?" one of the men asked.

"They didn't tell me, and you don't need to know," Stillwater replied. "Now, stop gabbing and get to work."

"Yes, Sergeant," came the reply.

The men continued to work at their tasks, oblivious to what the future held for them. Teams moved back and forth from a row of Conex containers near the railroad tracks. Removing cots and setting them up in rows inside the tents, it was obvious to anyone that a large group would be occupying these tents. Just who was the question on all of their minds.

A knock at his door startled Barstow out of his thoughts. "Yes, what is it?"

"Mr. Barstow, the convoy you were waiting on has arrived," the woman at the door said.

Walking out of his office, Barstow muttered a thank you and went toward the front entrance of the school.

Leaving the building, he was delighted to see a large number of U.S. government 5-ton trucks, all painted in the flat black that identified them as FEMA vehicles, carrying the men he was waiting for and what appeared to be a large amount of equipment. Two black HMMWVs also accompanied the trucks.

Stepping out of the lead HMMWV, a short, stocky man emerged. He was dressed in the black uniform of the FEMA Guards with black soft-side boots, the pants bloused over the top of them in a military style.

That must be Colonel Harrigan. Grinning as he adjusted the round plastic frames of his glasses, Barstow approached the man. With a voice as loud and enthusiastic as he could make it, he said, "You must be Colonel Harrigan. Welcome to Wausau. How was traffic?"

Removing the wrap-around sunglasses he was wearing, he looked at the man approaching him. Returning the smile, he extended his hand and said, "You must be Rick Barstow. I'm Wayne Harrigan. Travel from Madison was good."

The two men shook hands and turned to look at the line of trucks as the guards began to dismount from the vehicles and mingle amongst themselves.

"How many men did you bring, Colonel?" Barstow asked.

"I have 50 men and most of the equipment they will need. We'll forage for more, and another five trucks are due later in the week bringing the rest of our equipment."

"Excellent. I have the remaining National Guard soldiers erecting tents for the refugees we have in the camp. Once that is finished, we'll move them into those tents and your men can move into the buildings. Winter will be here in a few months, and we need to make sure they are comfortable. I know I wouldn't want to live in a tent."

"What do you plan to do with the National Guard people?" Harrigan asked.

"They aren't armed; we don't allow them weapons after the last group deserted. We'll round them up and put them in one of the tents," Barstow replied easily.

"They won't be a problem?"

"I don't think so. They've been pretty docile since we took their weapons. Their leader, a Sergeant Stillwater, said he understood that the desertion created an air of distrust."

"Air of distrust." Harrigan smirked. "What is he, a school teacher or something?"

"I understand he was a high school history teacher at one time."

"Interesting," Harrigan replied. "You have two other camps in town?"

"Yes, at two of the local high schools. That's where we house our more resistant guests."

"You don't think we should move these soldiers to one of those camps?"

"We'll see. For now, I think we'll leave them here."

"You're the boss," Harrigan replied.

"Shall we go inside for refreshments, and I'll share with you our situation here as well as up in Antigo," Barstow said.

"Ah yes, our Major Wolfe and the rebels. A pain in the ass for those in Madison."

"A pain in mine, too. Colonel, if you'll follow me."

CHAPTER 17

*"The true soldier fights not because he hates
what is in front of him,
but because he loves what is behind him."*

—G.K. Chesterton

Rahn and his team had left before the sun came
up, that period when false dawn's sun, still
below the eastern horizon, gives off a soft glow.
He had added two of Jake's guys to the team at
Jake's request.

I stood in the barnyard, along with Addie, Gary,
Brian, and Sam watching them drive across the
field and into the woods. As they disappeared
from sight, Addie leaned into me. "I'm scared,
Dad," she said.

I was startled by her words. She had never called
me dad before. Brian saw it and grinned. I put

my arm around her and said, "They'll be okay, Addie. Rahn's a good leader and Craig is smart. They'll be back."

"I'm sure they will," she said, but she sounded unconvinced.

I gave her a squeeze. "Let's go in the cabin and see what's for breakfast."

"I'm not real hungry right now," she replied.

"You should eat. It's good for you and…" I stopped myself before I finished the sentence. No announcement had been made, and it wasn't my place to do so. Brian had noticed my incomplete sentence and I was thankful he didn't say anything.

"Okay, sure," she answered and started toward the cabin.

"Before you go, *Dad*," Brian said, emphasizing the word dad, "Sam and I need to talk with you."

"Go on ahead, Addie," I said. "I'll be there shortly."

She walked off, her head down in a dejected way.

I turned to Brian and Sam. "What do you need to talk about now?"

"John, I have an update on the horde in Shawano," Sam said. "The last transmission I had heard said it was a nightmare. The mob has gone into a frenzy, burning everything, killing people, and generally raising hell."

"Lovely. Another frikkin problem," I remarked.

"This shit is starting to get out of control," Brian added. "We need to end this crap with Wolfe and FEMA, and start looking south for more help. If that horde comes this way, or even a part of them does…"

"Right now, it looks like they are following 29 toward Wausau; it will be their problem to deal with," Sam concluded.

"I feel guilty saying this, but better them than us. We don't need the added stress," I said.

"True, but we can't say for sure some of them won't come this way," Brian added.

"We'll focus on that after we take care of Wolfe. We don't have the resources to do more than that right now," I replied. "Sam, can you get ahold of Peter Corn over on the Rez and give him a heads up? The horde'll have to go through there before they get to us."

Sam bobbed his head. "I can do that. I'm sure it will make his day. It may get some of his fence-sitters off the fence."

"Yeah, he'll need them. We can't afford to lose Jake and his men. I'd understand if they left and went home. I would. Brian, speaking of Wolfe, what's the plan?"

"I think we need to hit him again hard and end this. The scouts have said he's beat down and his men look ragged and worn out. They can't be that good; it's only been one night," he said with a less than respectful tone.

"Okay, before you do that, let's get Linda up to speed. She's the only medic we have until Donna comes back. She won't be happy about it."

"She getting skittish?" Sam asked, giving me a sidelong glance.

"Only in that she's worried for her boys. She understands why we are doing this," I replied.

Sam nodded in agreement. As he walked back toward the barn, I heard him say, "I'm glad somebody understands."

*　　　*　　　*

The start of a new day did little to calm Wolfe's anger and frustration. He was down to two vehicles following yesterday's attack. Today would be payback. He had assembled his small force before breakfast, having asked Edmiston to wake them. Holding the meeting inside the headquarters building made sense to him; everyone was sleeping there until another building could be made ready.

"Good morning, men," he began.

The men were still waking up and were dog-gedly listening to his words.

Pointing at one of them, Wolfe said, "You, get your weapon and go down and relieve the sentry. Tell him to get back here pronto."

"Yes, Major," the man replied as he picked up his M4 and left the building.

Wolfe turned his attention back to the men in the room. "Today, we are striking back. We will enter that little town. What's it called again, Edmiston?"

"Lake View, Major," Edmiston answered.

"Yes, we'll enter that town and we will burn what's left of it. We'll draw those traitors out and end this once and for all."

The room was silent. The assembled men glanced at each other in disbelief.

One man decided to speak up. "Major, they have automatic weapons, and we know they have more than the two vehicles we have. They also have more people. We can't do a stand-up fight."

"There you are wrong," Wolfe replied, a sharp tone in his voice. "They won't send everyone. The fire will draw some out to investigate. We'll ambush them, steal their vehicles and weapons. Either the gunfire will draw the rest out, or we'll use what we have and find them."

"What if we take prisoners, Major?" one of the men asked.

"We only need one prisoner. After he tells us what we need, there will be no prisoners." The reality of those words sunk in quickly, even as tired as they were the men understood what Major Wolfe intended.

A slamming of the door interrupted the meeting. "Major, he's gone, sir."

"Who's gone?" Wolfe asked the man who was supposed to relieve the sentry.

"Wilson. Wilson is gone. There's a lot of blood out there, too."

"Dammit," Wolfe exclaimed.

*   *   *

"What's your plan, Brian?" I asked as we walked toward the cabin.

"Just a repeat of what we did yesterday, only this time we stay on target until they are all gone."

"What are our assets?"

"Two Hummers, two SAWS, and more than enough men. They can't have many left, and the two boys watching across the road took out the sentry. I got the call before we said good-bye to Rahn and his people."

"And you're just now telling me?" I asked testily.

He glared at me. "I just now had the chance. It's not your mission, Dad. It's mine."

"So what, you're pushing me out of the picture here?"

"I didn't mean it that way. Shit, you said I ran this unit, and I'm running it. We tell you what we're doing."

"I'm tired and I'm cranky," I said. "When is this going down?"

"Within the hour. They're loading up the Hummers and getting equipment ready. I'll offload the grunts just before the entrance, and then we'll race in with the Hummers and SAWs as shock troops. The grunts will mop up on foot."

"I'm guessing everyone knows what to do. You still need to let Linda know, but I think you should leave her here. She's not a combatant."

"I wasn't going to take her along. There will be no survivors. I'm not leaving anyone behind who can come back later."

"It's your show," I answered.

"Changing the subject," he said with that damn grin of his, "why is Addie calling you dad?"

I gave him a sideways glance. "You'll have to ask her."

*   *   *

Rahn and his team arrived in Antigo by mid-afternoon. They had left the main highway near the Langlade County Airport and headed north, going across country, avoiding small built-up areas and any possibility of being seen. The going was slow as Rahn had sent two men on foot to act as scouts as well as early detection of any surprises from the last time they were here.

Rahn chose to deviate from his original plan of using the Container company grounds as an assembly point. The new location was open, and the nearby woods had a nice clearing in the middle which afforded better concealment.

Stopping the small band, Rahn sent out two soldiers to listening and observation posts. The odds were low that they would be seen, as there were few people still in town with the majority either moving away to join families or in the refugee camps. Never the less, he wanted to be cautious.

"Everyone, gather round please," Rahn said.

The group shuffled over to him—Johnson, Craig, Jake's two men, Billy and Carl, Sajan, Jake, and Donna.

"I'll brief Hart and Roop later," Rahn began. "Donna, you and Johnson will stay here. I'll lead the team out about midnight. Craig, you and Jake will be close with me. Then, Jake's men, followed by Hart, Sajan, and Roop. We're taking the same path as before."

"And that is?" Jake asked.

"We'll cut through these woods, parallel to Rusch Road, by using the businesses north of it as cover until we cross Highway 47 by the hair studio. There's a patch of woods behind it. We can use those woods to get to another grouping of trees behind the Best Value Motel, and those woods lead behind the back of the armory. When we enter those woods, we'll go low and slow. They should have at least two sentries patrolling outside the armory. I want to observe their pattern with the NVGs first. Once we know how they are moving, Craig, you and Jake will quietly approach them, go through the empty Conex's in the back. You'll wait for the opportunity and remove the sentries."

Rahn paused and looked at Craig and Jake. "You two up for this? It isn't easy taking someone out with a knife."

Craig nodded his head.

Jake smiled and said he'd have no problem. "Killer here and me will be fine," he said, putting his hand on Craig's shoulder.

"Okay, then. Once they signal us that the sentries are out, we'll move in, enter the armory by the side door, raise hell and get out. We will not use stealth to get back here, but we will follow the same route. As soon as we enter the treeline, I'll do a quick headcount, make sure we have everyone, and then we'll beat feet back here. If we have no casualties, we'll hop in the vehicles and head home."

"Which way are we taking back home, First Sergeant?" Johnson asked.

"That road that we crossed before we entered here," Rahn said, pointing toward the east. "That connects to 64. When we hit 64, Johnson, floor it and well, get home as quick as possible."

"Are we driving by the hatchery?" Jake asked.

"Good question. I had forgotten we have visitors there. So no, we'll go cross country and head into the cabin area the same way we left it. Any other questions?"

Silence told Rahn there were none.

"Okay, then. Everyone, take time to catch some sleep, check your equipment, and eat something. We have these fine meals Uncle Sam provided for us," Rahn held up a tan MRE pouch. "Johnson, in about an hour, you and me will relieve Hart and Roop. I'll brief them then, and they can get back here."

"Yes, First Sergeant," he replied.

The group broke up. Craig and Jake gravitated to a spot next to the tire of one of the HMMWVs. Jake sat down, using the tire as a backrest. He smiled at Craig and said, "Snooze, ya lose."

Craig laughed and sat down across from him. Opening up his MRE pouch, he didn't even bother heating it by using the heater inside the MRE.

"What did you get?" Jake asked.

"I got shredded beef in barbecue sauce, black beans in seasoned sauce, jalapeno cheddar cheese spread, tortillas, oatmeal cookies and…"

Interrupting him, Jake chuckled and said, "Boy, you're gonna be able to fart those sentries to death, you won't need your knife."

"I ain't never used a knife on a man before," Craig said as he opened his shredded beef and put it on a tortilla shell with some of the cheese spread.

"From what your old man says, you ain't done a lot of things before this shit all started. Rahn must think you can do it, too. He picked you for this."

"I know, pressure's on, I guess," Craig replied.

"Just do what you have to do, and remember you want to get back to your pretty girlfriend. That's all the motivation you need."

The two men ate in silence for a while, each using the tortilla shells that came in their MRE.

Jake had chicken chunks, corn, cheese spread, and beef sticks to make sandwiches.

Craig broke the silence. "Why does it have to be like this, Jake?"

"Like what?"

"FEMA doing what they're doing, all of that. I get the hungry people but the bikers, that looter gang, the people I killed when Dad came to get us. Some of that I don't get. A lot of it makes me angry, and sometimes I get into a rage about it."

"Yeah, I get the hungry people, too. The other animals are just that—animals. I remember when I was in the army, they told us that civilization would break down in three days. That all of us were basically animals who were being controlled to behave a certain way because of society. When society goes, so goes the controls," Jake said.

"Well, that sure as hell *is* what happened."

"Now these FEMA types, just like the bikers, they're the ones that want to be in charge and will do anything. They see themselves as better than the rest of us, and they'll kill and worse to be that," Jake continued.

"What those FEMA boys did to that young woman's family was despicable and shows you how far they'll go. Some of the Guard soldiers say they're doing that in the camp in Wausau, too."

"Then, we should go there and stop them," Craig said absently.

"Don't say that to your old man, it'll give him ideas. I'm not wanting to fight no war if I can help it. Besides, we don't have enough people to do that."

"I know, but we should think about it. Somebody's gotta help those people."

Jake pursed his lips together, then said, "You can't save the world, Craig. All you can do is take care of your own."

*   *   *

Brian stopped the two-vehicle attack force about a quarter-mile from the hatchery. Ahead, he saw the two scouts waving at him from the right side of the road just before the entrance to the grounds.

He got out of the vehicle and waved his arm in the air, signaling the men in their vehicles, less the drivers and gunners, to assemble on him. He waved for the scouts to join him.

"We'll go in using two squads in a line," Brian said. "One right and one left. We won't move forward with the vehicles until you guys are in the entrance, so stay out of the way. We're going in hot. Follow us at a trot and clean up what's left.

I don't want any prisoners and no one gets away, either. Any questions?"

"Where do you want us?" one of the scouts asked.

"Just follow the squads. Do what they do and don't get shot. I don't want Jake pissed at me."

"You don't want my mom pissed at you, either," the scout replied jovially.

Brian returned his comment with one of his patented grins. Then, looking at each man present, he said, "Let's do this."

He got back in his vehicle and said to the driver, "Wait till they are on the road to the hatchery and follow them. When the vehicle behind us makes the turn, gun it."

"Yes, Sir," the driver replied.

"You ready up there, Owens," Brian shouted.

"Ready, Chief."

Brian watched as the two squads of soldiers rounded the turn into the hatchery. Pulling the charging handle back on his M4, he said, "Let's go."

*   *   *

Wolfe stood still for a moment, processing what he had just heard. One of his men was missing, most likely dead, and everyone in the room was looking at him. The sudden roar of heavy vehicles and the unmistakable sound of automatic weapons made him react.

"Get out there and stop them. We're being attacked," Wolfe yelled.

Three men jumped up and started out the door; the third one didn't even clear the doorway before they were gunned down in a burst of automatic weapons fire.

The remaining men fell to the floor as bullets ripped through the wooden walls of the building.

Wolfe lay on the floor, his hands over his head. Chips of wood and other debris fell around him as bullets ripped through the building. Glancing quickly around the room, he noticed Edmiston crawling toward the back of the building.

"Edmiston, where are you going?" he shouted.

Edmiston waved him over as more and more bullets rained into the building, tearing large chunks out of the walls.

Wolfe crawled to Edmiston. "Where are you going?"

"There's a back door here, Major, and we can get out that way."

Wolfe looked at his remaining men, all on the floor cowering in fear. The growing pools of blood by two of them indicated they'd been hit and were probably dead.

"Lead the way," Wolfe said as he followed Edmiston out.

They exited the building and ran for the trees beyond. A quick run of about fifteen yards got them into the woods and away from the conflagration behind them. The gunfire into the building was relentless. Wolfe stood just inside the tree line and watched, horrified, as his men were cut to pieces by the heavy machine gun fire going into the building.

"Major," Edmiston yelled. He was pointing to the left toward where the vehicles had come from. "We've got to get out of here, Major. We can't win this."

A look of resignation filled Wolfe's face before he nodded, and he and Edmiston ran deeper into the woods.

CHAPTER 18

*"Whoever fights monsters should see to it
that in the process he does not
become a monster."*

—Friedrich Nietzsche

I was sitting with Sam in the barn while waiting for word from Brian. We were too far away to hear anything, although I occasionally thought I heard gunfire. It was more than likely my imagination.

Sam wanted to scan other frequencies to see what he could learn about our growing problem in Shawano. I asked him to leave one of the radios set to our frequency, the one Brian had on the SINCGARS, and let him see what else he could learn.

My pacing must have bothered him, because he plugged in a headset and put it over his ears. I was in desperate need of a cigar and a drink. It was too early for the drink, but I was seriously considering the cigar when the squelch on the radio broke the silence.

"Base, this is Assault force, over."

I grabbed the handset. "Assault force, this is Base, over."

"Base, mission accomplished, over."

"Assault force, can you give me a SITREP, over."

I wanted a situation report; I needed to know everything was okay and not just the sterile radio communication that they did what they'd set out to do.

"Base, I have ten, I say again, I have ten enemy KIA, over."

That was good news; we took ten of them out of action permanently. "Assault force, SITREP on friendly forces, over."

"Base, we are all a go, over."

Some things in the army never changed. A 'go' was good and it meant no casualties. A no-go would not have been good.

"Roger, Assault force. Good job, over."

"Base, the top tar— is not pres—, over."

The transmission had not come in clear. "Assault force, say again, over."

"Base, the top target is not, I say again, is not present, over."

"Roger, Assault force. Base out."

That could only mean one thing. Wolfe had gotten away. He was still out there, and still a threat.

*   *   *

The radio operator took off his headset and raced out of the communications room down a long hall to Rick Barstow's office. Knocking rapidly on the door, he waited to be told to come in. Opening the door, he saw Barstow and the new arrival, Colonel Harrigan sitting comfortably in chairs, drinking coffee.

"Yes, what is it," Barstow said in a voice it was apparent he did not appreciate the interruption.

"Sir, we just intercepted a radio transmission from those people by Antigo," the radio operator explained.

"Which people?" Barstow asked impatiently.

"The traitors, sir. They just attacked what we think are our men. It sounds like most of them are dead, but some may have gotten away."

"What?" Barstow bellowed, standing rapidly, spilling his coffee. "Attacked where by who?"

"I think it was Major Wolfe's people, sir. The transmission said the mission was accomplished, they had ten enemy KIA and that the primary target was not one of them."

"Son of a bitch." Barstow threw his now empty coffee cup across the room. "Ten dead?"

"Yes sir, that's what it said," the operator confirmed.

"It would appear the Henrys and your man Rahn are a more formidable enemy than we thought," Colonel Harrington said casually.

"Colonel, I need you to go up there and fix this," Barstow said firmly.

"Oh, I will, I will. I need to communicate with Madison first. They need to know what is going on, and I'm not taking a crew of mostly unblooded people up there without them knowing about this first."

Barstow looked incredulously at the colonel. Collecting himself, he glanced at the radio operator and said, "You can go now. Close the door as you leave."

*   *   *

The victors and their spoils returned to a grand celebration. Brian was in the lead Hummer when it pulled into the barnyard. His two-vehicle team was trailed by two all-black HMMWVs. Hopping out of the front seat of his Hummer, Brian said, "It was a cakewalk, Dad."

"Cakewalk? Are you old enough to use that term?" I asked as I hugged him.

Brian smirked. "They were almost asleep when we showed up. Most of them were trapped in a wood frame building that looked like it was made for the military during World War II."

I remembered the architecture well—small buildings with white clapboard siding and green shingled roofs. Poorly insulated, so no matter the season you were uncomfortable.

"Wolfe got away," I said, confirming the transmission.

"Looks that way. He wasn't there when we looked through the bodies. One of the guys thought they saw two people running into the woods but couldn't be sure. We didn't pursue them."

"Probably should have," I said. "Of course, that's Monday morning quarterbacking."

Brian gave me a look but didn't say anything.

"I see you got two more vehicles," I quickly added.

"Yeah, plus several cases of ammo and MREs, weapons, a couple of radios and boots," he replied.

"That's good," I said. "Boots?"

"We took them off the dead. No sense letting good equipment go to waste and we'll need the boots over time."

A loud CRACK followed by a "Woo-hoo" traveled through the gathering. Jumpy soldiers instantly put weapons into a ready position, searching the area for intruders and targets.

"What the hell," I said.

"You got him," a child's voice shouted.

Brian and I took off at a run toward where the voices had come from. As we raced behind the cabins toward the field, I could see three boys; Mike, Ethan, and Caleb. Ethan held up a turkey by its legs and he was struggling with it. It was a big turkey, especially being held next to a young boy of age six.

"You got him good, Mike," Ethan said.

Brian and I got to the boys. I was panting a little, but I had run faster than Brian had. I looked at them, hands on hips.

"Look what Mike shot, Mr. John," Caleb said before I could yell at them. It took the wind from my sails.

The two Haines boys had taken to calling me Mr. John. Linda felt they were too young to call an adult by their first name and I didn't care, so we settled on her way.

"That's a nice turkey there, boys," Brian said.

Sucking in a lungfull of air, I asked, "Mike, what did you shoot it with?"

Holding up his Savage single shot Bolt Action .22, he replied, "This, Grandpa."

I had been afraid he had taken one of the shotguns. As hard as that would have been to believe, each of the boys were very respectful of guns. We had them around everywhere, but now I had to wonder.

"That's an impressive shot, Mike," I said. It's hard enough to shoot a turkey with a shotgun, so when a nine-year-old can get close enough to shoot one with a .22, that's special.

"Won't be long before you join us as a sniper," his proud dad said.

As we were congratulating the boys, we were suddenly surrounded by two moms and two older men. Linda and Nancy had gotten to us. Nancy was much more agile of late and rarely needed her walking stick. Sam and Gary, both bending over and gasping for air because they weren't in as good of shape had also joined us.

"What happened?" Nancy asked. She did not sound happy.

"The boys got a turkey," Brian said, grinning.

"That's good shooting," Linda remarked. "You two are supposed to let me know where you are," she added, her arms folded across her chest and those furrows she got on her forehead when she squinched up her face, trying to look mad.

"Sorry, Mom," Ethan and Caleb said together.

"But, looook at this turkey," Ethan quickly added.

Nancy started to laugh.

I don't know if it was the release of stress or the comedy of the moment. Regardless, her laugh was contagious because before I knew it, everyone was laughing. Gary was laughing and complaining that he couldn't breathe, which made me laugh harder. In the middle of us stood the three boys wondering if we had lost our minds.

Mike cradled his rifle in the crook of his arm, exactly like I'd taught him and said, "C'mon guys, these people are crazy," and he led Ethan and Caleb to the cabin.

As the laughter ended, Sam and Gary said they were going back to the barn and left the four of us alone.

"You should have been watching them, Brian," Nancy scolded.

"How was I supposed to do that? I was on a mission," he responded, the pitch in his voice a little higher than usual.

"No excuses," Nancy said.

I could see the mischievous look in her eyes, but I don't know if Brian could. It was fun watching him squirm.

She turned and walked to the cabin. Brian quickly followed, and I could hear him pleading his case.

"The boys are very proud of themselves, aren't they," Linda said to me. We were the last ones standing there in the tall grass watching Nancy and Brian walk away.

"Wouldn't you be," I replied.

"Wild turkeys are good eating," we said together and then laughed at the common expression.

"You wouldn't have a spare .22 or two around, would you, John?" Linda asked.

"Sure, I have three in the basement gun cabinet."

"Ethan's been asking for one, and I was wondering."

"I'll get him set up later today if you'd like."

"That'd be nice, thank you."

"No problem. I know if I was his age and just about everybody had a gun, I'd want one, too. What about Caleb? If I know brothers—" I recalled the issues vividly with my brother and me when one of us got something the other didn't.

"He's too young, but he is going to have a fit," she replied.

"What about a crossbow?" I asked, not certain if the snark was recognizable.

"Ha, I'd rather he have a gun."

I nodded my head in agreement.

Without another word, she headed to the cabin.

*   *   *

Wolfe and Edmiston stumbled through the forest and dense underbrush. Neither of them was armed. Scratched from the branches and brambles whipping across their exposed skin, they were sweaty, dirty, and tired.

"Where are we heading to, Major?" Edmiston asked.

"The armory. There's nothing back there," Wolfe said, gesturing behind him with his head. The smoke off in the distance and the abrupt end to gunfire was a clear signal that his force, what there was left of it, had been wiped out. *This is guerilla warfare, and the Geneva Convention and Rules of Engagement no longer apply.*

"We need to keep going and not stop. Thomas can get together a team and come out here for

any cleanup that needs doing. I'll get reinforcements from Wausau," he continued. "This is
getting out of hand. No one can expect me to
defeat well-armed terrorists with a handful of
untrained men."

"Yes, sir," Edmiston replied, a hint of relief in
his voice. "How far do you think we have to go,
Major?"

"Twenty miles as the crow flies, maybe a little
less."

"How long do you think it'll take to get back?
Neither of us have eaten."

"We'll find something along the way, I'm sure,
Edmiston. Until then, it's one foot in front of the
other. We should get there by early morning."

"That's a long time, Major."

"You'll live, Edmiston. If you don't, I'll kill
you." Major Wolfe started laughing at his own
joke.

Edmiston just stared at Major Wolfe.

Wolfe kept his thoughts to himself. *This man is
insane. I've got to get out of here. Maybe I should
kill him myself. Blame his disappearance on the
terrorists.*

*   *   *

"Just squeeze the trigger," I said to Ethan.

CRACK! The .22 let out its sharp sound and the paper target got another hole in it.

"Good shot," I said.

He smiled and turned toward me, the muzzle of the rifle following Ethan and aiming at me.

I reached out and grabbed the muzzle, still warm from the round, and pushed it toward the field. "What did I say about pointing a rifle," I gently said. This was why I'd always started youngsters out with a single-shot weapon.

"Sorry, Mr. John, I forgot," he said, a scared look in his eyes.

"Just remember next time, okay?"

"I will," he said, his eyes now downcast. I could tell he was really sorry.

I had spent the afternoon with Mike, Ethan, and Caleb. I was teaching Ethan how to use the .22 that I had taken from the basement. His younger brother Caleb was understandably upset that he didn't have his own rifle, but I'd let him shoot Mike's. The world would have ended had I let Caleb shoot Ethan's rifle.

Mike didn't seem to mind and was enjoying playing the role of an older brother. It was a nice diversion from all that was going on around us. The boys were having fun, and to be honest, I was probably enjoying myself more than they were.

I heard a crunch of feet behind me and turned. Linda was watching us.

"Who's having more fun here?" she asked. A rather astute woman she was sometimes.

"Me," a child and one manly voice chimed.

That caused her to laugh.

I was sitting on the ground and had to roll over to push myself into a squatting position before I could fully stand. Took me a second after standing to make sure I wasn't dizzy. A brief lightheadedness told me that I needed to get into better shape.

"You alright?" Linda asked, concerned.

"Yeah, I stood up too fast," I answered, taking a step back from the kids. "Ethan's a quick learner," I added, quickly changing the subject.

"He's really taken to it," she said. "The only guns he had before…before all of this were nerf guns and super soaking squirt guns."

"We had a moment or two of where *not* to point the weapon. That's part of why these single shot bolt action .22s are good for learning," I said. "He gets it. Now, Caleb, that one is going to be a handful. Very adventurous and hard-headed."

"He comes by it honestly," she answered with a smile.

"I know."

"I have to get back. I've got work to do. I just wanted to check and make sure they weren't driving you crazy," she said.

"They're fine. All three of them are fun to be with. Relieves the stress in a good way."

"If you say so, John. Or what is it you guys say? It's your lie, you tell it?"

"It's true. I love kids, got some of my own, you know." I grinned.

"I really have to go. Gotta make hay. You boys listen to Mr. John, you hear me?"

"Yes, Mom," Ethan and Caleb replied together.

*   *   *

It was close to midnight, and Rahn had gone back to the assembly point to wake everyone who was still sleeping. He roused each man by kicking their boots. He stood over Donna and whispered her name a couple of times, then said, "Miz Henry, it's time."

Donna sat up from the sleeping pad she'd been laying on, rubbed her eyes and said, "Thank you, Chris."

Sure everyone was awake, he said in a low voice, "Final equipment check. Make sure your weapons are loaded and on safe. Only the point man will be ready to fire. If you forget anything, we won't have it when we get to the armory. So *don't* forget anything."

The men shuffled around as they checked their equipment. Most of the men carried an AR, a few had shotguns. All wore MOLLIE vests, complete with plate carriers, a ballistic insert meant to protect them from small arms fire and shrapnel. A partial moon gave some light, and while the men were primarily shadows, Rahn could tell who each of them was.

As they finished, he brought them together for final instructions. "Okay, from this point forward, we are silent. Hand signals only. Keep your fingers off the trigger of your weapon. Make sure nothing is rattling and pick your feet up when you walk. Johnson."

"Yes, First Sergeant."

"When you hear the fun and games starting, you be ready. If it gets too noisy, you get to that hotel, the Best Value Place, and we'll come out of the woods here."

"You want us to bring both vehicles?" Johnson asked.

"I'm sure Miz Henry can drive a Hummer, but we'll all just pile in the one and haul ass back here if it comes to that. Miz Henry, if that happens, listen closely. If you could, start the other vehicle, because we'll be coming out hot and will have to leave rather quickly."

"No need to be so formal, Chris," Donna said. "I know we'll have to get the fuck out of here if that happens."

The broad grin across Rahn's face was one of both amusement and admiration.

Jake and Craig checked each other's equipment. After they were satisfied, Jake said, "You gonna go talk to your mom before we head out?"

"Yeah, I guess I should," he answered. Picking up his M4, Craig stepped over to where she was sitting.

"Hi, Mom," Craig said sheepishly.

"I was wondering if you were going to come talk to me. I guess you didn't want the others getting on you about it."

Craig half-shrugged. "They all know you're my mom."

"I know. Can I get a hug?"

Craig reached over and hugged her. The equipment on his vest made it awkward, but they managed. "I'll be okay," he assured her as they pulled apart.

"Just be careful, Craig."

"I will, Mom. I promise."

"Alright people, time to go," Rahn interrupted, and the team headed off into the darkness.

"He'll be okay, Miz Henry. Craig's a good guy and he knows what he's doing," Johnson said as they watched the team disappear into the night.

"I know. You can call me Donna."

"You're a mom. I can't call you by your name."

"Okay, Specialist Johnson," she said with a grin.

They settled in to wait…and pray.

*   *   *

The day had been reasonably quiet. Brian led his men in inventorying the weapons and ammunition. We were sitting pretty good with what we had. Nevertheless, I was still concerned if we kept having these fights, we'd run out of ammo. Rahn couldn't just go to the Supply office in Wausau and requisition us more. I knew we'd have to find another source.

The raid in Antigo wasn't meant to be anything other than a warning raid meant to send a message; get the hell out of our home and go back where you came from.

The next closest place was Wausau, about 70 miles away. As far as I knew, it was well fortified. We weren't going to raid them and get away with anything but casualties.

I was still worried. It appeared we had to either send a very strong message to keep out—one I did not think would be listened to—or resort to raiding supply convoys to Wausau or what I was certain was a similar FEMA operation in the Appleton-Green Bay area. We'd had no contact with anyone over there and had no idea what was happening, except for the golden horde burning and raising hell. It would make sense to have something overt that way if these FEMA people were intent on controlling everyone and everything.

It was dusk, and Brian, Nancy, and I were sitting on the porch enjoying the quiet. I'd apparently worn the boys out shooting, because they were all in bed asleep. Max and King, my faithful guard German shepherds, were snoring on the far end of the porch. Linda was inside working, which is what she did a lot of. She never seemed to stop working, and I wondered if she was either hiding from us or was obsessive about something else.

Brian and I were sitting next to each other in the two chairs on what was known as *my* side of the porch. I decided I'd take pity on him and share a cigar and some whiskey.

Nancy had made him sit by me. "You two sit over there and pollute the planet. Those damn cigars stink, and you aren't sitting by me and smoking one, Brian Henry."

Of course, Brian being the professional smart ass he is turned to me and said, "That's how you can tell she's mad and serious, Dad. When she uses my whole name. Then, there is the *I'm going to need to hide* name."

"You need to hide name? You mean your full name," I asked, pretending to be serious.

"Yup, Brian Matthew Henry. When she calls me that, I hide."

"So you admit it, do you," Nancy said in mock accusation. "You always say you don't hear me. Now I know you're hiding, like a coward."

"Oh Nancy darling," Brian said sweetly, again using a mocking tone I knew was going to start another battle here on the porch. "You know I was kidding, sweety."

"Yeah, right, Brian. Just kidding," she answered back.

Then just like that, everyone got quiet. The crickets started chirping as dusk began to overcome us, getting darker. We each sat there with our thoughts.

"What do you think they're doing?" Nancy finally asked. 'They' were the 800-pound gorilla in the darkness.

"Sleeping," Brian said as he took an exaggerated puff from his cigar and blew the smoke out in front of him.

"How can you sleep when something like this is going on," Nancy asked, a hint of frustration in her voice.

"I can't explain it," Brian replied. "You just do. You lay back, close your eyes and clear your head. The next thing you know, someone is kicking your boots, telling you it's time."

"You make it sound so simple," she said.

"It isn't. It's dealing with the moment. You're scared, and then you're not, and then you are again. You're a mad man destroying everything in front of you, and then you stop because a puppy wandered into the battlefield."

Nancy glared at him. "Don't mock me, Brian, I'm serious."

"So am I. It happened in Baghdad. We'd been attacked with an IED and then engaged in a firefight. Somebody's puppy wandered into the road and we stopped shooting. The Hajis didn't. They don't like dogs. They shot the puppy. We shot them."

"I don't understand any of this," she said softly.

His smirk had vanished and he gave her a tender look. "It's hard sometimes, but remember when that biker tried to grab Mike here in the yard. You didn't think, you just reacted. It's the same way."

"I don't want to remember that day," Nancy said. "It's too terrible of a memory."

I'd stayed out of this discussion and silence returned as we sat there, now fully cloaked in the darkness. Brian and I slowly puffed on our cigars as Nancy stared at the fireflies in the yard. The moon was bright and our expressions still visible. I watched the two of them. They were lost in their own thoughts, and they needed that.

A creak of the screen door brought all of us out of our trance. Linda stepped outside and stopped without closing the door. "I'm not interrupting anything, am I?"

"Gosh, no," Nancy said. "Come join us."

"Here, Linda, you can have my chair," Brian commented as he stood and winked at me.

"Thank you," Linda said as Brian sat on the steps and she took over his chair. "Is this my whiskey?" she asked as she held up a glass.

"You can have my chair, but you can't have my whiskey," Brian said quickly as he hopped over and snatched the glass out of Linda's hand.

"Would you like some?" I asked her.

"No, thank you. I was just being mischievous." She giggled.

All of us here on the porch were relaxed even though we knew we had friends and family 20 miles away getting ready to go into harm's way. I don't know if that meant we were becoming numb or immune to our situation, or if we were doing a good job of hiding our anxiety, but the time spent here tonight was a welcome break from all of the other nastiness we'd been dealing with. The four of us chatted for a while, mostly about normal things like gardening, Linda's herbs, and Nancy's culinary expertise.

Then, Brian stood up from the steps, his cigar done some time ago, stretched with great dramatic exaggeration and said, "Nancy, you ready to go to bed? I'm tired."

Standing up herself, she'd given up on the walking stick a few days earlier as she no longer needed it, she said, "Good night, you two. John, if you hear anything, please let us know. I know you aren't going to bed yet."

"I will," I answered.

Nancy didn't often call me John, preferring Fil instead. She was worried, but the grin Brian gave me when he walked by toward the front door said a lot, too.

Asshole, I thought. I knew exactly what he was thinking.

"G'night Dad, night Linda, night John Boy," he said as he entered the cabin through the screen door.

All I could do was shake my head. At times I thought he wasn't quite right. At other times, I knew this was how he managed stress. It worked and rarely did anyone get mad about it. Putting my son's antics out of my head, I focused on Linda.

"It's nice out here," Linda said, breaking the silence.

"It is," I replied.

We both sat there, neither of us talking. The night's sounds were getting louder, owls and crickets were prevalent with the occasional high-pitched whine of nature's terrorist, the mosquito, screaming in my ear.

"Think the corn will be good this year," Linda said.

I didn't respond and the silence returned for what was probably five seconds before she burst out laughing. I joined her about two seconds later.

"What are we so afraid to talk about?" I asked.

"I think we both know, but I also think it's best we not go there," Linda replied.

"I'm not ready for it, either."

"There's no rush, and now isn't the time or place. Not now."

"Maybe someday," I said.

"So, how about that corn," she said as she placed her hand on my arm and squeezed.

"How about that corn," I agreed.

*   *   *

Rahn and his team made it to the woods behind the armory. He had Hart low crawl up to the edge of the woods, and with his NVGs, keep an eye out for the sentries or any changes that may have occurred since their last visit.

Gathering the rest of the team in a small circle about twenty yards from Hart, Rahn repeated the instructions for the raid.

"Jake and Craig, you two remove the sentries, no gunfire. If we shoot, the mission is blown."

Both men, visible in the moonlight, nodded their heads in agreement.

"Once the sentries are down, drag them out of sight. Wave us in, and we'll assemble behind the building. Once we are together, we'll go in using a line formation. We'll go through the door and I'll take the lead. Behind me, in order, will be Roop and Billy. Then, Hart followed by Carl, Craig, and Jake. At that point, Roop will break off and set the explosives on their vehicles. Once he waves to let us know those are set—Roop, 2-minute timers."

"Yes, First Sergeant," Roop whispered.

"We'll breach the door. I'll take Billy to the common room and Hart will lead his team to the assembly hall. I'm going to toss a grenade into the common room and when it goes off, Hart and his team will violently enter the assembly hall. There, you will toss two grenades, unload one magazine, reload, and withdraw. We'll quickly exit the building and assemble behind it, do a quick headcount, and move back the way we came. Any questions?" Rahn made eye contact with each of the team members.

No one spoke—the determination and nerves of the moment took hold, keeping the men silent.

"Okay, gentlemen. Let's go."

*   *   *

Wolfe was exhausted. They had stumbled through the woods, over fences, and gotten hung up in old barbed wire fences. He was tired of listening to Edmiston ask him if they could stop and rest. *If we stop, I'm falling asleep and I can't do that.*

Ahead, they saw a slight glow and Wolfe said, "Stop."

Edmiston almost fell down on his hands and knees at the barked order. "What is it, Major,"

Edmiston gasped as he lay on the ground, his uniform torn, sweat-soaked, and dirty.

"That light up ahead looks like a house."

Edmiston rolled over on his back, panting in the dark. "If it's a house, then there are people, sir. We have no weapons, what are we gonna do?"

"If it's a house, then there has to be a garden. A garden means food."

At the mention of food, Edmiston perked up. "We can't just walk up there. In our uniforms, those people might shoot us. Hell, sir, they just might shoot us anyway."

"Edmiston, it's simple. We get closer to the house and we wait till the light goes out. Then, we find the garden, grab some veggies, and get back in the woods."

"What if they have dogs?" Edmiston was too tired to continue being military-like polite.

Wolfe was too tired to correct him."We'll wait and watch. If they have a dog, we'll know."

"Okay," Edmiston gasped. "We'll wait; good idea."

"Follow me. Let's get closer and watch. Maybe we'll see the garden before they go to bed. That will make it easier."

The two men slowly made their way to the edge of the woods and the yard around the house. The white clapboards of the house glowed in the night. The dim yellow light inside, obviously from some kind of lantern, gave a good indication that whoever was in there was awake. Kerosene for lanterns was in short supply and no one would waste it by leaving a lantern lit all night.

"Take a break, Edmiston. You sound like you need it."

Edmiston waved his hand and flipped over on his back, panting heavily as he struggled to breathe.

"You sound like a damn freight train, be quiet."

"Yes, sir."

Wolfe heard Edmiston lightly snoring. *The son of a bitch fell asleep.*

Extending his leg, Wolfe kicked the man's boots, causing him to stir. The snoring stopped.

Wolfe located a garden between them and the house. He could see it clearly. *I hope whatever is in there is ripe enough to eat.*

It was then he noticed the light inside the house had gone out. *Won't be long now.*

Wolfe had no idea how long he sat there, but he caught himself falling asleep. He reached over and shook Edmiston awake. "Wake up. It's time to get dinner."

With a groan that was far too loud for Wolfe's liking, Edmiston rolled over and pushed himself into a sitting position. "In a few minutes," he whispered.

"Do you know what's in the garden, Major?"

"I'm not psychic, and I don't have night vision eyes. We'll have to crouch low, go over there and see."

"Any dogs?"

"Haven't seen any. Let's go." Wolfe stood up, crouched over, and ran toward the garden, Edmiston right behind him. The heavy thud of their boots was the only sound in the darkness.

Wolfe stopped and dropped to his knees, Edmiston followed next to him. They were at the edge of the garden.

Not fenced in, the garden was easy to access. What looked like cucumbers or zucchini were growing on the edge. Tomatoes, in that stage that was somewhere between red and green, were right next to them. There were also pole beans.

"Take your shirt off," Wolfe ordered the man.

Edmiston slowly unbuttoned his shirt and handed it to Wolfe. Spreading it on the ground, Wolfe began to take the closest vegetables and put them in the shirt. It didn't take him long to clean out all of the plants near them.

Balling the shirt up like a bag, he whispered, "Let's go to the other side of the yard to get back into the woods. We'll go a bit until we are far enough away that we can eat this."

"Yes, sir," Edmiston whispered. The excitement of having something to eat was evident in his enthusiastic response.

Crouching over, they raced across the yard and to the safety of the trees in the distance.

CHAPTER 19

"You may have to fight a battle more than once to win it."

—Margaret Thatcher

"**A**ntigo Base, this is Wausau Base, over," said a voice.

The radio operator half asleep in his chair sat up straighter. "Wausau Base, this is Antigo Base, over."

"Stand by for a message, over."

"Roger, standing by," said the sleepy operator.

"Go get Sergeant Thomas," the senior radio operator said.

The sleepy operator rose from his chair and left the communications room. He hurried down the hall to the small office Sergeant Mark Thomas occupied. Knocking on the door, he heard a muffled, "Yes, what is it."

"Message coming in from Wausau, Sergeant. We thought you'd want to hear," the operator said through the closed door.

*   *   *

"I'm on my way," Thomas replied as he sat up.

Searching the floor for his boots, he found them by touch and bent over to put them on. Finishing without tying them, he pulled the laces tight, stood and shuffled down the hall and into the communications room.

"What kind of message," he said with a yawn.

"We're waiting on it now. Kind of unusual for this to happen at almost 2 a.m."

"I agree," Thomas mumbled as he searched for a chair to sit in.

Finding a straight back metal desk side chair, he pulled it over and waited along with the two operators. A few moments later, the breaking of squelch through the radio startled all three men awake.

"Antigo Base, this is Wausau Base. Message follows, over."

"Wausau Base, this is Antigo Base, send message, over," said the senior operator.

"SITREP as follows. Your Advance Party near Lake View has been attacked twice. I say again, your Advance Party near Lake View has been attacked twice. Unconfirmed reports indicate casualties are significant. No contact with Advance Party leadership. Be advised that a party from this base will arrive at your location by 1200 hours today to begin new operations, over."

"Wausau Base, this is Antigo. Roger," the operator replied, stunned and clearly shaken at the news. Turning toward Sergeant Thomas, he said, "Sergeant, I don't understand."

"It means those men at the hatchery are most likely dead. It means our shits in the wind and we are in trouble. That's what it means," Thomas said with a bit more angst than he knew he should. He stood. "I need to double our guard and get you people looking better than you do now. I have no idea who is coming, but I'll bet money on it that the person is senior rank to Major Wolfe."

"What do you want us to do, Sergeant?" the senior operator asked.

"Square this office away and stay on that radio. I'm sure we'll know more soon."

*   *   *

The corn we were growing was going to be a nice crop. It seemed every time Linda and I experienced any kind of silence during our time on the porch, we brought up corn. Anyone walking by would have thought we were both drunk because one of us would say, "So, how about that corn," and we'd erupt in to laughter.

Linda had finally excused herself, saying she had work to do in the morning and needed to get to bed. The entire time we sat there, her hand never left my arm.

The homestead, as I sometimes called it, was a different place at night. Especially when even the bugs went silent. There was still the occasional sound of an owl and sometimes the cry of a hungry animal, but it really was a different place at night.

I sat there wondering about Craig and the assault he was on. It was too much to hope that it would go as simply and smoothly as Brian's had. We'd been very lucky during all of this. All we'd lost was Quint, Carol, and Grady. I could also count Emma in that, and of course Charlie and the entire Winston family. I held little hope that the count would stay that low for long. I had a premonition that at some point, we'd lose a lot more people.

I stared up at the stars in the sky, not so very different from the sky I had looked at before this all started, and sighed. That sky had borne witness to all that we had done and would bear witness to what we would do. I sometimes wished the sky could talk, talk in a way we understood. It would help me understand. Our world was changing, and not for the better it seemed.

*   *   *

Craig and Jake made it to the Conex behind the armory with little effort. It appeared neither of them had been seen by the two sentries, who were aimlessly walking their route, paying little attention to anything as their eyes were focused on their feet, as if they thought they might stumble over something.

Dropping low to the ground, Jake and Craig crept closer to the sentries.

Craig held Brian's Ka-Bar in his hand in front of his body, the blade running along the length of his arm.

As they watched the two sentries round opposite corners of the armory, both men glanced at each other and nodded.

Craig ran quietly to the corner of the building, knowing Jake was at the other corner. They would wait for the sentries to come back around and then take them. He could feel his heart pounding in his chest as he stood, his back tight against the wall. It wasn't a small building, and he knew it would be a bit before the man came back around. Craig used the time to get his breathing under control and calm his nerves.

Breathe slow, just like Jake said.

He heard the man approaching and he readied himself.

He saw the man and moved, pushing the sentry's weapon away. Shoving him down on the ground, Craig clamped his hand over the man's mouth and slashed his neck.

Blood flew up, splattering Craig, momentarily disorienting him. The man thrashed and gurgled. Jake had told him that slashing the throat would sever the windpipe.

The man thrashed about under Craig's grip. Putting the man out of his misery, Craig stabbed him in the side where his plate carrier did not offer any protection. In a moment, the man stopped moving. Craig lay there, panting.

A tug on his leg made him jump. "You okay, Craig," Jake whispered.

Craig nodded his head but didn't move.

Jake reached down and grabbed him by the back of his Improved Outer Tactical Vest and pulled him off of the dead man. "We gotta go. I already signaled Rahn."

Craig nodded again.

"You did good," Jake whispered. "Let's go."

Craig took a deep breath. "I've never done that before," he said as he glanced at the body lying on the ground.

"You did it like a pro," Jake said. "Let's go; they're waiting." The two men trotted off toward Rahn and the rest of the assault team.

Rahn was waiting as the men, their backs pushed tight against the rear wall of the armory, prepared themselves mentally for the next phase, taking their places in line behind Carl and Hart.

Carl gave the men their weapons as all Craig and Jake had with them were the knives.

Rahn gave them a thumbs up and whispered, "Okay, Roop, when we round the corner, you go do your thing at the vehicles. When you give us a thumbs-up, come back here and wait. We'll go in, raise hell, and come back out."

Roop nodded his understanding.

"Hart, when we go in, my team will take the left wall, and you take the right wall. You will parallel us down the hallway, weapons at high ready."

Hart replied, "Roger."

"No shooting until Billy and I blow the common room. Then, throw your grenades, empty your magazines, load, and get the hell out." He moved a few feet down the line and said, "Jake, I want you to stay by the door and keep it open.

I don't need us banging into it as we try and run out."

"Okay, Chief," Jake replied. "No Three Stooges routines on the exit."

Rahn smiled and moved to the front of the line. He glanced back at his men, raised his arm, and waved them forward.

*   *   *

Thomas left the communications room and went to the assembly hall. Turning on the overhead light, he shouted, "Get up, people. We got work to do."

No one moved but audible groans from the men broke the silence.

"I said, get up," he shouted.

The men slowly moved about, grabbing their boots and clothing.

"You people get dressed and stand ready. I'll be back and we can get started."

Out of habit, Thomas reached for the light switch, stopping himself at the automatic movement. Smiling at the action, he headed down the hall to his room to get his equipment and weapon.

*   *   *

Rahn stopped at the door and motioned for Roop to move out for his part of the mission.

The soldier trotted across the blacktop, his boots barely making an audible sound. He stopped at the first vehicle, opened the door and placed his Semtek charge inside, then made sure the timer was set.

He went to the second vehicle and repeated the operation. Stepping back, he turned to face Rahn, gave him a thumbs-up, and trotted back across the blacktop toward the corner of the building.

Rahn looked down his line of men, nodded and placed his hand on the door handle. Opening it, he lead the teams inside.

As planned, the teams lined themselves against the walls and moved slowly but purposefully down the hall, their weapons pointing in the direction they were moving, fingers next to the trigger.

"Fuck," Rahn muttered a few feet into their journey.

*   *   *

Thomas went down the short hall from the assembly room and turned the corner. Seeing something out of the corner of his eye, he looked to his right.

Coming toward him were two lines of soldiers, their weapons pointing at him. *Not* his men.

"Damn," he said and jumped back toward the assembly room.

As he ran, he shouted, "Take cover! We're being attacked!"

*   *   *

Shouting to his team, "Move, Now!" Rahn quickly ran forward, the teams following him.

Hart rounded the corner leading to the assembly hall, kneeled down and reached into his vest, taking out a grenade. Carl, standing behind him, pointed his weapon toward the open doors in front of them.

"Shoot, God Dammit," Hart yelled.

Carl began shooting, joined a few seconds later by Craig.

Pulling the pin on his grenade, Hart tossed it toward the open doorway and then started to fire his AR-15.

Craig and Carl emptied their magazines and reloaded, the unfamiliar action taking Carl a few extra seconds.

Boom! A loud explosion from the room in front of them momentarily caused them to stop shooting. Then, the men inside the assembly hall began shooting back.

A loud *Smack* in front of Craig caused him to jump as Carl fell like a ragdoll to the floor.

Craig squatted low and grabbed Carl by the back of his plate carrier and drug him backward. Seeing a large hole in Carl's head instantly told Craig the man was dead. He aimed carefully and shot towards the open door. Firing with one hand, he dragged Carl around the corner and toward the exit.

*   *   *

A large *BOOM* shredded the room. Inside the hall, Thomas pressed his body tightly against the wall.

"Fire, Fire," he shouted.

The men who had not been injured in the grenade blast followed his orders. They aimed automatic fire down the hall, their bullets going everywhere.

I'm air force; I didn't sign up for this army shit. Thomas continued to shout at the men to fire as the roar of the weapons became almost deafening. *We've got to get control of this situation.*

"Shoot, God Dammit, Shoot!" he yelled, and the men in the hall began to respond with more rapid-fire. Shooting into the doorway through the cloud of debris from the grenades, the men increased their generally aimed fire toward the only entrance to where they were.

*   *   *

Hart reached for another grenade but felt a thump and fell backward. His vest had stopped the bullet. It hurt like hell, and he gasped for breath. He heard Rahn's voice shouting, "Get up, move!"

Hart crawled on his back and made it around the corner, Rahn covering him with rapid-fire from his M4. The noise inside the building was deafening as gunfire was exchanged between the two groups.

A sharp blow to his left arm caused Rahn to drop his weapon.

"I'm hit," he said. With his right hand, Rahn reached down and picked up his weapon, following Hart, Billy, and Craig out the door.

Racing around the building, Craig handed Carl off to Jake, and the group ran for the woods.

Halfway to the tree line, an explosion sounded, followed quickly by another blast. Roop's handiwork had been successful.

They reached the assembly point and Donna quickly patched up Rahn. It was just a grazing wound about as big around as his pinky finger and maybe a quarter of an inch deep. He knew he was lucky. Another half-inch and he could have had a much more serious injury, possibly fatal given their limited medical resources. They put Carl in a poncho, placing him in the back of one of the HMMWVs and drove home. The mood on the trip back was somber.

*   *   *

Wolfe awakened with a start. Disoriented, he wasn't sure where he was. Then the memories of the last 24 hours led him to where he currently was. He and Edmiston had eaten all of the vegetables they had gathered from the garden and had fallen asleep.

Wet from the morning dew, he wiped his hand across his face where he found a slime trail left by a slug that had made its way across his face during the night.

Extending his leg, he kicked Edmiston's boots and said, "Wake up."

Edmiston stirred but did not awaken.

Wolfe kicked him again, only harder. "Wake up."

"What?" Edmiston said with a sleep-filled voice. "What?"

"Get up. We have to move."

"How far do we have to go, Major?"

"Not far. I figure less than an hour or two."

"Good," Edmiston remarked. "I could use a shower, change of clothes, and real food."

"Right now, if real food was an MRE, I'd gladly eat it," Wolfe replied. "Get up. Let's go."

*   *   *

Using the wall to support himself, Sergeant Thomas stood up. His ears were ringing from the explosions and the rifle fire inside the assembly hall. He patted himself down looking for wounds. Other than his ears, he was uninjured.

I don't imagine the VA's going to increase my disability over this.

The other men in the room were not as fortunate. Almost all of them appeared to be wounded. Going over to offer first aid, he slipped on a large pool of blood spilling out of two of his men. Both were obviously dead. A few more had shrapnel wounds from the grenades. Two men just looked wounded but the blood on them was from the others.

"You two, help these men as best you can. I'm going to see where the guards are and send a message to Wausau," Thomas explained.

A short distance outside the doorway, he saw two dark stains on the floor. Blood.

Good, looks like we inflicted some damage.

In his room, he put on his vest, grabbed his weapon, and stopped at the communications room.

"Notify Wausau that we have been attacked," Thomas said. "Preliminary casualties are two dead and four wounded. More information to follow."

"Okay," the senior operator said. His shaking voice indicated he was still nervous about the firefight that happened just a few yards away from the room.

As he went down the hall, Thomas could hear the operator calling, "Wausau Base, Wausau Base, this is Antigo, over."

Approaching the outer door, Thomas stopped to listen. Pulling the charging handle back on his M4, he set the selector switch to burst, ensuring that if he had to engage that every time he pulled the trigger, the weapon would fire three times. Holding the weapon in his right hand by the pistol grip, he pushed the breaker arm on the door and stepped out into the night.

He was stunned. His only two vehicles were twisted and burning. *Damnit.*

He didn't see any signs of his two guards, and fearing the worst, he began to search for them.

It didn't take Thomas long to locate their bodies. Both dead, weapons and equipment stripped from them.

They had enough people to do this and get away. Damn, we're in trouble.

*　　　*　　　*

Johnson and the other driver drove Rahn and his weary team home. Donna took Rahn into the large cabin to properly clean and dress his wound. On the ride home, she'd assessed everyone else of any injuries.

Rick shouted the Hummers were returning as he saw them across the field.

Addie burst from her cabin and raced to meet the team. As they disembarked from the vehicles, she saw Craig. She ran toward the HMMWV only to stop and stare in horror at his blood-covered face and clothing.

"Addie," he called. He ran to her and told her he was okay, that the blood wasn't his.

She looked him over carefully. Addie had become a tough woman, but it took her a few minutes to accept he wasn't injured.

Jake had lost one of his people. He knew he had to take Carl home, but first, he had to gather his team and explain why they needed to stay in the fight.

*　　　*　　　*

After making sure Craig was okay, I went to see Jake and put my hand on his shoulder. I'm not a natural hugger, but I felt my hand was as good as a hug. The grim look on his face spoke a thousand words.

Jake looked at me and I could see the hurt in his eyes. "John, it's all a game till somebody dies. Now I have to take Carl home to his people. I have a tough journey to make."

"You want to use my truck?" I asked, squeezing his shoulder with my hand.

"Yeah, I'd appreciate that," was his softly spoken reply before he turned and walked away. He found Billy, and the two of them removed Carl's poncho-covered body from the back of the HMMWV.

Gary stood in the doorway of the barn watching. Kicking the ground and making a small dust cloud, he went over to the two men.

"Jake, I can build a coffin for him. Nobody needs to see him wrapped up like that."

"Thanks, man," Jake said. "Billy and I will get him cleaned up. No one needs to see him like this, either, and I know his ma is going to want to say good-bye. I can't stop her from doing that, wish that I could."

I watched as the two men shook hands, and Gary went back into the barn to begin his unpleasant task.

Me, I felt guilty. I was glad it wasn't my son.

*   *   *

Entering the communications room, Thomas saw the senior operator there. The other two operators he'd learned were in the assembly hall helping. "You get ahold of Wausau?"

"Yeah," the operator replied.

"I have an update. We have two more KIAs and both of our vehicles have been destroyed."

"Geezus," the operator remarked. "One of the wounded I hear probably won't make it, either."

"Damnit," Thomas said under his breath. "Send the message. I'll be in the hall if you need me."

Thomas left the room to check on what was remaining of his men.

*   *   *

I joined Addie and Craig, asking him if he was okay. His demeanor was subdued. He'd been through a lot since I'd picked him and Donna up in Appleton. His world had quickly and remarkably changed; all of our worlds had changed.

All I could think of were the words from the Emily Dickinson poem, "To See the Summer Sky". It came from a book a friend of mine had given me years ago, "To see the Summer Sky. Is Poetry, though never in a Book it lie—, True Poems flee—." Shit just definitely got real now.

Summer was over, and if it wasn't real before, shit had just definitely got real now.

I looked at my youngest son. "I heard you carried Carl out of the armory."

"Yeah," was Craig's reply.

"I'm proud of you," I said.

"I don't feel real proud right now, Dad."

"I understand. Still, I'm proud of you and I…" The emotion stopped me from speaking, the words catching in my throat. I reached out and hugged my son.

"Dad," a voice said from behind me. It was Brian.

I let go of Craig, and was barely out of the way when Addie took over.

"Let's get you out of those clothes and cleaned up," she said.

I turned my attention to Brian. "What," I said, a bit too harshly. It didn't faze him.

"Sam needs you."

"Why, what now?" I asked.

"He has some information you should hear, and Owens up at the bunker said we have new refugees."

"We don't need any refugees; we can't *take* any more refugees," I said sharply.

"They're from Shawano, Dad. I've seen them; they look like shit. Nancy made some soup. She and Linda are out there with Owens and two of my guys feeding them."

"Damnit, Brian," I said through gritted teeth.

He stopped me before I could say more. "Dad, these people were burned out of their homes. When you hear their stories, you'd agree to help them, too. We are still human beings. We can't just turn them away. Besides, they were heading toward Antigo. What do you think would have happened to them there?"

He was right, of course. He knew I knew he was right, too. I changed the subject. "What does Sam want?"

"We need to go up there. Too much activity here," he answered.

We went into the barn and up to Sam's new home—the loft. He had even put a cot up there so that he could hear any traffic that came over the radio when he needed to rest.

Once we entered his room, I wasted no time. "What do you have to share, Sam?"

"Hey there, John. Unfortunately, nothing good, but maybe it isn't all bad."

"Gimme the worst of it," I said, sighing as I sat on a stool in front of the rack of radios.

"Seems there's a new FEMA chief in Wausau, and he's heading to Antigo," Sam said.

"Barstow get canned?" I asked. "That would be good news."

"Better the devil you know. I don't know if Barstow was canned or not, but the radio chatter I've picked up on says some guy, a FEMA colonel named Harrigan arrived in Wausau with a lot of troops."

"Shit, how many?" Brian said.

"That I don't know. He radioed before the raid, said he was going to Antigo and should be there sometime this morning. When Antigo told Wausau they'd been hit and hit hard, he said he was sending reinforcements and equipment. He would accompany them."

"Lovely," I quipped. "Any word on Wolfe?"

"The last transmission from Antigo said he'd arrived this morning with one other."

"Hmmm… Looks like Wolfe has nine lives. This Harrigan guy, a colonel. That mean anything to you, Brian?"

"Nope. Could be one of those FEMA titles or he could be National Guard peeps that turned."

"I'll ask Rahn if he knows him. If Rahn doesn't, that could be a clue. If he's just FEMA, that could be a positive." I looked at Sam. "What's the other bit of news you have?"

"I've been monitoring calls from a group that says they're National Guard and are looking for Rahn. Claim they are from Rhinelander."

Brian smirked. "They're asking for Rahn by name?"

Sam nodded. "Yup."

"What do you think?" I asked Sam.

"Could be legit, but I thought all the Guard went to Wausau. Why they're looking for him, I haven't heard."

"Maybe Rahn knows," I said as I stood up.

"What about the refugees, Dad?" Brian prodded. "We can't turn them away."

"No, you're right. We can't. There are some buildings still standing in Lake View. Let's get them settled in there and see what we can learn. That damn horde has me as worried as FEMA does."

"Some of them are armed and we have a few extra weapons," Brian said.

His words stopped me cold. "Armed?" I asked.

"Yeah, hunting rifles and wheel guns. Nothing significant. They're pissed, too."

"We're gonna need people, Brian. Our little team is down by one now and we can't do this all by ourselves. Jake's taking Carl home, and I suspect he'll take one or two of his people with him."

"I think they'll fight. Who they'll fight remains to be seen," he replied.

"Well, let's feed 'em and get them housed in town," I said. "I'll go meet them later and feel them out. See whose side they're on."

CHAPTER 20

*"What we call our despair is often only the
painful eagerness of unfed hope."*

—George Eliot

Colonel Wayne Harrigan rode in the lead HM-MWV as it moved up Highway 45 toward the south side of Antigo. He led a small convoy consisting of two 5-ton trucks, a dozen FEMA troopers in each one, and a second HMMWV trailing the convoy. He had enough ammunition, rations, and fuel to last him and his men five days. A second convoy from Madison would bring more in a tanker with 16,000 gallons before the five days was up.

The steady hum of the tires on the blacktop road lulled him into a relaxed sleep state.

"Colonel, we're almost into town," the driver of his HMMWV said, startling him into the present and the mission ahead.

"Thank you, son. It's pretty country up here, easy to get distracted."

"Yes, sir. I grew up not too far from here, a bit north, near the Cisco Chain of Lakes. I had to get out of here, found out I'm more of a city boy than a Northwoods boy."

"We'll get you reintroduced to the Northwoods, son. Antigo is no city, and we will be out in the field doing what we need to do to bring this situation under control."

"Yes, sir," the driver said. *Great. I thought I had a good job driving for the colonel and I find out he thinks he's Daniel fucking Boone.*

The convoy entered the town, driving past every fast food joint known to man and abandoned taverns and bars seemingly on every corner. All empty. They continued north, past the fairgrounds and an old funeral home, and then crossed Highway 64.

"The armory should be just up ahead, sir," the driver remarked.

Harrigan didn't respond, already thinking about what he was going to say to Major Elias Wolfe when he met him.

The driver turned onto Amron Road by a deserted Chevy dealership and then about one-hundred yards later pulled into the armory.

Two still-smoking black hulks of what used to be FEMA HMMWVs were in the parking area.

"Pull over next to those, driver," Harrigan ordered, pointing at the two mangled piles of metal and burnt rubber.

"Yes, sir."

As the vehicle stopped, Colonel Harrigan got out and gestured toward the rear of the armory yard. Following his signal, the two 5-tons' drivers parked there.

The second HMMWV stopped near Harrigan, and Lieutenant Nelson King stepped out. Saluting Harrigan, he said, "Sir, what would you like me to do?"

"King, get those vehicles unloaded. I want all the ammo and equipment inside. Get the men inside as well, but give 'em some time to stretch their legs. Then, come find me. I'll be chewing Major Wolfe's ass."

Smirking slightly, King saluted and said, "Yes, sir."

*   *   *

Rahn was sitting at the kitchen table wearing a brown t-shirt with his ACU pants bloused in the top of his tan combat boots. His left arm was bandaged and in a sling, held tight to his chest. Sitting near him were Nancy, Donna, and Linda. In his right hand was a clear glass tumbler, a brown liquid in it.

"You day drinking now, Chris?" I asked as I came into the room.

"It's medicinal, for the pain," he replied, looking up at me.

"Just where did that come from," I asked to no one in particular, but my eyes focused on Linda.

"I gave it to him," Linda said. Her tone was one of authority, as if to say how dare you question our helping this wounded man.

"Uh-huh," I said, choosing to say no more. I wasn't going to win this one. Time to hide my stash better. "You know anything about a guy named Harrigan out of Madison?"

"I've heard of him," Rahn answered. "I think he was Air National Guard. Why?"

"Seems he is the new head of the FEMA guys in Antigo."

"He's air force, so how much can he hurt us?"

My thoughts went immediately to Carol. She'd been a U.S. Air Force vet and she had guts. She hadn't been afraid of a fight, either. "I don't know," I said.

Walking over to the table, I took one of the remaining empty chairs and sat down. I stared at the glass in front of Rahn.

Linda noticed and said, "You aren't in pain. You can wait till this evening."

I guess my look was funny because everyone at the table started laughing.

"It's my damn whiskey," I said and immediately regretted it. All three ladies chastised me for my heartless hoarding. I took my medicine, choosing to save the fight for another time.

"What about the National Guard in Rhinelander?" I asked as I strategically changed the subject.

"No one there. I mean, there is an engineer unit there, but they never came in when all of this started. I know their first sergeant, a guy by the name of Charlie Yerks. He's a Gulf War vet. Got a Purple Heart and Silver Star on one of his deployments. Why do you ask?" Rahn asked.

"Sam picked up a radio transmission. They're out looking for you by name."

"Hmm, that could be a good thing if they have people. We didn't know if they went rogue or what happened. A lot of the smaller guard units never showed up, seemed to disappear. It was on my list of places to visit, but—"

"Sounds like it's worth following up on," I interjected. "I'll have Sam look into it."

"I can take a team and check it out," Rahn said.

"That's probably a good idea. Once your pain is under control and you heal a bit," I said.

That got me several harsh looks from the women. Changing the subject quickly, which I was getting good at, I said, "Donna, has Craig talked to you about anything?"

"No, just normal stuff. Why?" she asked.

"You should talk to him. You really should," I insisted.

Getting up from the table, she headed toward the door briefly stopping to ask, "Is everything alright?"

"Oh, it's just dandy," I said with a grin.

"Okay, John." She stared at me suspiciously and left.

"I have a headache," I said. "I need something for the pain."

"I have some processed willow bark, it's basically aspirin. I'll get you some," Linda said.

I tried very hard not to roll my eyes as I watched Rahn stifle his laughter.

*   *   *

Harrigan stormed into Wolfe's office. "What in the hell were you thinking, Major?"

Wolfe sat at his desk eating an MRE. He glanced up. "Oh hello, Colonel Harrigan, sir." Setting his spoon down, he stood up. The two men had met briefly in Madison before Wolfe was promoted to major.

"You have seriously fucked up," Harrigan said sharply. "No guards, everyone inside one building, and you lose all of them, your equipment, everything!"

"I had a guard out, sir," Wolfe replied defensively. "Those people took him out and then attacked."

"One guard. One fucking guard in hostile territory, and you'd already been attacked once. Are you stupid or incompetent?"

"Sir, I resent that implication," Wolfe retorted.

"I don't give a good goddamn what you resent, Major. It wasn't an implication; it was a statement."

Wolfe shut up and just stood there.

"I should relieve you and send your sorry ass back to Wausau to guard prisoners and refugees." Taking a breath to calm himself, Harrigan continued, "I'm not going to do that. I need people, shooters. We are going to end this. Am I clear, Major?"

"Yes, sir," Wolfe replied.

Harrigan narrowed his eyes. "So, this is what we're going to do…"

*   *   *

"A baby?" Donna shouted. "You're going to have a baby? Oh, my lord. Oh my."

"Mom, it's going to be okay," Craig said somewhat defensively.

"I think it's wonderful," Donna said. *Wonderful and scary all at the same time. This is not the best time for this to happen to any of us right now.* But putting her best face on, Donna said, "I'm gonna be a grandma."

"Yes, you are," Addie quickly said. "I need your help, Mrs. Henry. *We* need your help."

Softening her expression as she looked at Addie, Donna said, "We have time. How far along do you think you are?"

"I don't know. I've missed two periods, so I guess maybe three months?" Addie said.

"We have time. Six months is plenty of time. It will go fast, but we have time," Donna repeated, trying to sound encouraging. "There's much we need to do. I need to see what kinds of vitamins we have and ask Linda about herbal solutions."

Standing up, Donna hugged Craig and then Addie. "I'll go talk with Linda now," she added.

"We're going to get married, Mom," Craig said, stopping her. "It's the right thing to do."

"We'll get that taken care of, too. Addie, why don't you come up to the cabin later and we'll talk about how we are going to get you through this pregnancy and the wedding."

"Yes, Mrs. Henry," Addie said, smiling.

"Please, call me Donna."

"Okay," Addie said, pausing. "Donna."

*   *   *

Sam tried to raise the Rhinelander National Guard on the radio for most of the afternoon. It wasn't until evening that he finally made contact.

"Rhinelander, Rhinelander, this is Henry Base, over."

"Henry Base, this is Rhinelander, over."

"Rhinelander, stand by. Over," Sam said, putting his hand over the mic. "Allen, run get Rahn and John."

Allen got up from the box he was sitting on and raced out of the barn loft.

Panting as he reached the cabin, he saw John, Rahn, and Brian sitting on the porch deep in conversation.

Stopping to catch his breath, he said, "Rahn, Sam wants you and John. He has Rhinelander on the radio."

All three men jumped up and hurried to the barn.

Once upstairs, Rahn said, "You have Rhinelander?"

"Yup, they're here. Hold on a sec and I'll get them again," Sam said. "Rhinelander, this is Henry Base, over."

"Henry Base, this is Rhinelander, go."

"Rhinelander, how's your softball pitching skills?" Rahn said, having taken the microphone out of Sam's hands.

"Softball?" Sam asked.

"Yeah, we played a softball game against each other last year at Fort McCoy. He pitched terrible. We had something like five home runs in a row before his commander pulled him off the mound," Rahn explained.

"Henry Base, I still can't pitch worth a damn. Lots of home runs for you guys. Some of my people still give me a hard time about it."

"That's Charlie Yerks," Rahn said, putting his hand over the microphone. "This could be something good and at a good time, too."

"Rhinelander, do you remember where we last met?" Rahn said.

"Roger, Henry Base."

"Let's meet there day after tomorrow. Noon."

"Wilco, Henry Base. Rhinelander out."

"Henry Base, out," Rahn answered. Setting the microphone back on the table, he said, "There's a Best Western in Crandon. We met there for a meeting to coordinate some training for a drill weekend. We'll meet there and see what's up."

"John, you just might like this," Sam answered, meeting my eyes.

"I just might," I replied. "We may need the manpower."

"If they have any," Brian said.

"Let us hope they do, gentlemen," Rahn added.

*   *   *

Harrington had all of the men gather in the assembly hall. Strutting in, he had Sergeant Thomas get the men into a formation as he stood observing, Lieutenant King and Major Wolfe standing by his side.

Thomas spent a few minutes getting the men lined up into squads to look like a military unit. Once he was satisfied, he moved to the front of the formation and stood at the military position of attention.

Facing the men, Thomas called, "Group, attention."

The men, in varying degrees of speed, all mirrored what he did, standing straight, arms at their sides, feet together.

Pivoting around in what the military would call an about-face movement, Thomas stood still.

Harrington nodded and in a low voice said to Wolfe and King, "Follow me, men," and walked in front of Thomas. He stopped and faced Thomas.

Giving a military salute, Thomas said, "Sir, the command is formed."

Harrington saluted Thomas, who then did an about-face and marched behind the formation.

Harrington stood facing the men, King and Wolfe standing behind him.

"Be at ease, men," Harrington commanded.

The men relaxed their posture, none of them speaking as they watched their leader.

"Men, those of you who were here have had a rough go of it. We are going to change that," Harrington said.

The men began to look around, smiles returning to their faces.

"We will take the fight to the enemy. The next few days will be spent getting equipment ready, forming you men into teams that can work together, and preparing for taking aggressive action against these people and ending this lawlessness once and for all. Lieutenant King will be working with Sergeant Thomas to make that happen. Major Wolfe and I will be making the necessary plans and getting what we need from Wausau or Madison to help us accomplish our mission successfully."

The men began to stir, the newer arrivals starting to cheer. Soon, all of the men were cheering and shouting.

"To the victors go the spoils," Harrington shouted at the men. "We will be victorious, and you men will make that happen!"

The men, all raising their arms and cheering loudly, started to chant, "Victory, Victory."

Harrington smiled, turned to stare at Wolfe and said in a voice only loud enough for Wolfe to hear, "That, Major, is how you lead and inspire."

*   *   *

The mildly cool evening wrapped itself around me like a comforting blanket. Aside from some harsh winters, we had some of the most glorious weather imaginable. Most everyone was outside enjoying it. The bugs today were not that big of an issue, and that alone made being outside in the early evening tolerable.

I was headed toward the barn, no particular reason except the voices drew me there. Brian and Craig were chatting with Rahn as Sajan and Allen sat off to the side, observing. The National Guardsmen were doing what all soldiers do with their time off, playing grab-ass, throwing axes at a sheet of plywood, and chatting in small groups.

Before I made it to the barnyard, I glanced north, north toward the parallel lines of small cabins we had built, smoke rising from one of the chimneys and two young boys, Ethan and Caleb Haines, playing in what was quickly becoming a dirt road between the cabin rows.

I stood there, and if I closed my eyes, the smell of woodsmoke and the chatter of voices would have taken me to another time, a peaceful time.

With my eyes open, I saw what mattered. What we, together, had made from a tragedy that we were still getting used to. We were becoming a family—a large, somewhat odd family but a family all the same. We'd built our homes here and we'd defended them. We'd shed our blood for them and done what was necessary to survive and, in some instances, thrive. It was our home, a home worth defending and doing what we could for each of us. We'd accomplished much in a few months—more than I ever could've imagined.

Yet all was not tranquil. We weren't pioneers building a life together. We were hanging on by our fingernails. Men were out there who wanted to cause us harm. Those men wanted our freedom, our property, and for some of us, wanted our lives. If I ever needed a reason to keep going, to keep standing up for what was right, all I needed to do was stand where I was now, close my eyes as I smelled and listened to that around me. The motto of the U.S. Army, the other home I'd spent so much of my life with, is "This We'll Defend." That is exactly what we would do. We would defend it and each other. This was our home and no one would *ever* take it away from us.

EPILOGUE

The two men were enjoying their quiet time, sitting on the cabin porch, the scene of so much of their history over what was now almost a decade. The evening was just beginning and the gray shades that clothed this time of night were starting to show.

"I like this time of day," the younger of the two men said.

"Yeah, me too. John Henry liked the morning, said he could think best then," the other man replied.

"I remember him sitting out here when I'd get up. Him, his coffee and cigar."

"You were kinda young then. I'm surprised you remember," the older man answered.

"I remember a lot more than you give me credit for. I pretty much grew up here."

"Yep, you did," the reply came almost absent of any emotion. The older man let his mind wander… back to the beginning, when all of this started and the world began to change. His eyes misted as he thought about all those people they'd lost and who were now at rest in the field behind the row of small cabins.

"You okay," the younger one asked.

"Yeah, I'm just remembering—so many good times and bad times right here. Hard to believe some of it. Wouldn't, if I hadn't lived it."

"You figure out what you're going to tell Emma yet," the younger man asked.

"Nope. But I'm going to have to. Can't keep it from her forever."

HERE'S A SNEAK PEEK OF BOOK 4: *FIRE OF DEATH* BY D.M. HERRMANN

As Lieutenant Nelson King of FEMA strode into Colonel Wayne Harrigan's office inside the Antigo National Guard Armory building, he wore the standard black jumpsuit that all FEMA para-military personnel wore. His leg holster held a Browning 9MM pistol.

"Colonel, this is the sorriest collection of people that I have ever personally experienced," King announced.

Harrigan, seated at his desk, looked up from the papers he was reading. Dressed identically to King, the only distinction between the two uniforms were the silver eagles on Harrigan's collar and the silver bars on King's. Harrigan was the commander of the FEMA forces, sent into the area to deal with what they were calling an insurrection.

"What do you mean, Lieutenant?" Harrigan asked.

"That sergeant, Thomas is his name, has been moving these men through patrolling exercises straight out of the *Army Field Manual*. These men can't get their movements straight. They get into each other's lane of fire; they can't comprehend overwatch. They are a sorry lot, Colonel," King explained.

"Get me, Wolfe," Harrigan ordered. "And bring his sergeant along with him."

"Yes, sir," King answered as he turned and left the office.

He returned a few moments later, followed by Major Elias Wolfe and Sergeant Mark Thomas. Wolfe was a young man, about six feet tall and had tight curly brown hair. He was dressed in the standard black FEMA jumpsuit with black rubber-soled, high-top boots. Wolfe had formerly commanded the National Guard Infantry Unit based in the armory. He had moved to the FEMA Camp in Wausau and had been sent back to help with ending the insurrection.

Mark Thomas was of average build with blonde hair and sharp blue eyes. He, too, was dressed in the standard FEMA uniform. Like Wolfe, Thomas had also served in the military, having been a U.S. Air Force Security Police Officer. The three men entered Harrigan's office and stood in front of his desk.

"I would like an assessment of how the training is going," Harrigan began. "A way to get to the root of the issue that I learned in my military career was to start with the most junior person and work my way up the rank scale. That ensures no one is intimidated by rank or by their senior person. Sergeant Thomas, you start. How is training progressing?"

"These men aren't soldiers, Colonel. They don't know the basics. They've been thrown together and are expected to work as a team," Thomas said. "Some have prior military service, but they were mostly, like me, rear-echelon types. They don't know how to fight or act like a fighting unit. So, the training is very slow, Sir."

"Major Wolfe, what's your summation?"

"Sir, shouldn't the lieutenant go before me?" Wolfe asked.

"Wolfe, I've already heard from the lieutenant. And don't forget, in this mission, you are subordinate to him. I don't give a good goddamn about your rank. This is about skill and ability. Now, answer my question."

From the corner of his eye, King watched as Wolfe took a moment to calm down. It was clear Harrigan's words had hit him hard and he was not pleased.

"Sir, I agree with Sergeant Thomas. These men may be okay to guard a detention or refugee center, but they aren't combat soldiers. They haven't had that kind of training or experience, and it isn't in their DNA."

"In their DNA, Major?" Harrigan said, raising an eyebrow. "Explain."

"I should have been more clear, Colonel. They weren't trained to be combat soldiers, and most of them have never even been part of a sports team. They don't know how to behave," Wolfe explained.

"I see," Harrigan replied as he leaned back into his chair. Rubbing his chin with his right hand, he sat silently for a moment. Then, he leaned forward, resting his elbows on the desktop.

"How long do you need, Major, to turn these people into an effective force?" Harrigan asked.

"At least six to eight weeks, Colonel," Wolfe answered.

Harrigan's eyes traveled toward Sergeant Thomas and he fixed his gaze on the man. "And you, Sergeant, how long?"

"I agree with the Major, Sir. Six to eight weeks," Thomas replied.

Using his desktop to push himself into a standing position, Harrigan slowly rose to his full height, almost five feet eight inches. He leaned his stocky body forward across the desk. "You men have two weeks. I'm not running a basic training outfit. We are here to suppress an insurrection by military deserters and civilian criminal terrorists. Two weeks, gentlemen, and then we strike."

ABOUT THE AUTHOR

D.M. Herrmann is a retired soldier, having spent twenty years in the U.S. Army. Enjoying a rich, adventurous, and non-traditional army career, he draws on those experiences, crafting them into elements of these stories. He has authored three fiction novels under the pseudonym Evan Michael Martin. *To See the Summer Sky* is the third novel in his John Henry Chronicles series. He lives in Wisconsin.

CPSIA information can be obtained
at www.ICGtesting.com
Printed in the USA
LVHW031432310122
709622LV00001B/43